KIDS IN THE KITCHEN

By Kate and Tyler Metz
EDITED AND COMPILED BY HILDA COOPER

ATHENEAN PRESS

LOOK FOR THESE FINE COOKBOOKS BY HILDA COOPER

FAMILY SECRETS: A SOUTHERN HERITAGE COOKBOOK

KIDS IN THE KITCHEN
A Cookbook of Yummy Foods That Kids Can Easily Prepare

HOLIDAY TRADITIONS: A SOUTHERN HERITAGE COOKBOOK

MOTHER ESTELLE'S OLD SOUTHERN RECIPE DESSERT COOKBOOK

THE ULTIMATE BROWNIE, BAR & COOKIE COOKBOOK

MOTHER ESTELLE'S EASY HOMEMADE CANDY COOKBOOK

MORE COOKBOOKS COMING IN 2002 FROM ATHENEAN PRESS

BRIDE'S GUIDE TO FAKING IT
A Cookbook And Marriage Survival Guide

HOW THE HECK DID I END UP IN THE KITCHEN COOKBOOK

SOUTHERN PLANTATION COOKBOOK

SHOO-FLY PIE & APPLE PAN DOWDY
Over 250 Old Southern Recipes That Are Nearly Gone With The Wind

KIDS IN THE KITCHEN: A Cookbook of Yummy Foods That Kids Can Easily Prepare Copyright ©2001 by Athenean Press. Inc. All rights reserved. Printed in the United States of America. No part of this book may be used or reproduced in any manner whatsoever without written permission, except in the case of brief quotations embodied in critical articles and reviews. For information address ATHENEAN PRESS, INC., 2949 East Desert Inn Rd., Suite 1, Las Vegas, Nevada 89121-3607

ATHENEAN PRESS books may be purchased for educational, business, sales promotion or fundraising uses. For information, please contact: Special Markets & Promotions, ATHENEAN PRESS, INC., 2949 East Desert Inn Rd., Suite 1, Las Vegas, Nevada 89121-3607 or visit us online at www.AtheneanPress.com. On your letterhead, include information concerning the intended use of the books and the number of books you wish to purchase.

ATHENEAN PRESS and the Parthenon logo are registered trademarks of ATHENEAN PRESS, INC.

ISBN 0-9701466-9-8

Table of Contents

Getting Started........................... 1

Mixing It Up.............................. 2

Cutting Up In The Kitchen 16

Microwave Magic....................... 34

Something From The Oven 52

Now You're Cooking................... 90

Master Kid Chef 107

Getting Started
A Note to Kids & Their Parents

The kitchen is often referred to as the heart of a home because it is where love turns plain, ordinary things like eggs, flour and milk into magically delicious things like birthday cakes and pizza. It is also the most dangerous room in the house. Sharp blades, grinding motors, hot stoves and ovens and microwaves can be helpful tools but they can also be tools of injury and destruction.

<u>*Kids belong in the kitchen only when accompanied by a responsible parent or other adult*</u> –Someone who can help them learn to use the "magic" without being harmed by it. This book relies on parents to teach basic kitchen skills and safety rules to their children. We provide you with the fun, easy recipes that will take your child from simple mixing to complex multi-stage recipes. All are perfectly suited to both the talents and tastes of kids and teenagers.

Use this book as it is intended, not only as a great little cookbook, but as a source for quality time and learning between a loving, responsible adult and an eager to learn and talented child. Along the way you will build skills and memories that will stay with you both for a lifetime.

My Best To You Always,

Hilda Cooper

P.S. You may be surprised at how delicious these simple recipes are! Why not include some in your Holiday Party and Dinner Menus and give your child a head start on being a contributing player in creating new family traditions.

KATE & TYLER METZ with HILDA COOPER

Mixing It Up

What You'll Learn:
- How to combine, mix and blend foods

What You'll Learn To Use:
- Measuring cups, measuring spoons
- Electric mixer, blender, can opener, whisk, spoons, forks, mixing bowls

Some Safety Issues To Consider:
- Keep fingers away from beaters, inside blenders, blender blades and sharp can lids
- Parents or other responsible adults should supervise young people closely until skills are fully mastered

KIDS IN THE KITCHEN

AFTER DINNER MINTS

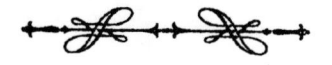

Ingredients:
1	3 oz	Package of cream cheese
3	cups	Confectioners' sugar
1	drop	Food coloring
1	drop	Mint flavoring

Beat cream cheese and add flavoring and food coloring. Mix in confectioners' sugar. Roll and knead well. Shape in small balls and flatten or put in flower molds. Can be made with different flavors and colors also. Vanilla, lemon, orange and almond are good choices.

BUTTER MINTS

Ingredients:
- 2/3 cup Sweetened condensed milk
- 7 cups Confectioners' sugar
- 2-3 drops Oil of peppermint
- 2-3 drops Food coloring
- 1/2 cup Butter
- 1 tsp Salt

Decorator sugar, if desired

Beat butter and salt together, until well blended. Add condensed milk. Add sugar. Remove from bowl and knead until mixture is well blended. Add flavor and colorings. Divide candy into several sections, if desired, to make several colors. Roll candies into small balls, dip in decorator or colored sugar, and flatten slightly.

CARAMEL APPLE DIP

Ingredients:
- 1 8 oz Package of cream cheese
- 2/3 cup Brown sugar
- 1 Tbs Vanilla extract

In a medium-sized bowl, beat together cream cheese, sugar and vanilla. If the mixture is too runny for your taste, add a little more brown sugar to the mixture. Serve with apple slices or banana chunks.

JUICY FRUIT TOWER

Ingredients:
- 4 each — Canned peach halves
- 4 slices — Canned pineapple
- 1 cup — Frozen whipped topping, thawed
- 4 whole — Maraschino cherries

Lettuce leaves

Cover four salad plates with crisp green lettuce leaves. Top each with a pineapple slice. Top with a peach half. Place a dollop of whipped topping in the hollow of the peach half, top with a maraschino cherry.

MARSHMALLOW FRUIT DIP

Ingredients:
- 1 8 oz — Package of cream cheese
- 1 7 oz — Jar of marshmallow crème
- 1 tsp — Coconut, vanilla or almond extract

Best together cream cheese, extracts and marshmallow crème until mixed thoroughly. Also excellent with pineapple or strawberry cream cheese.

MILLIONAIRE SALAD

Ingredients:
1	14 oz	Can of sweetened condensed milk
1/3	cup	Lemon juice
1	10 oz	Package of frozen whipped topping, thawed
1	8 oz	Can of undrained crushed pineapple
1	cup	Chopped nuts
1	cup	Maraschino cherries

Beat sweetened condensed milk and lemon juice together until smooth; fold in whipped cream topping, pineapple and nuts. Place in cut glass bowl. Top with maraschino cherries.

ONION DIP

Ingredients
1	pkg	Onion soup mix
2	pints	Sour cream

Combine ingredients until thoroughly blended. Refrigerate for at least two hours. Serve chilled with tortilla or potato chips or cut-up vegetables. Note: This recipe works well with almost any flavor dry soup mix.

TROPICAL FRUIT SALAD

Ingredients:
1	20 oz	Can of pineapple chunks
1	15 oz	Can of fruit cocktail
1	15 oz	Can of mandarin oranges
1	15 oz	Can of pink grapefruit sections
1	3 oz	Can of sweetened flaked coconut
12	whole	Maraschino cherries

Open cans, and dump fruit and juices in a large bowl. Sprinkle with coconut and decorate with maraschino cherries. Cover and chill for at least one hour. Serve chilled.

WHIPPED CREAM

Ingredients
2	cups	Heavy whipping cream
2	Tbs	Powdered sugar
1	tsp	Vanilla extract

Combine all ingredients in a medium sized mixing bowl and beat with a whisk or an electric beater until firm peaks form. Do not over mix. Serve on top of sweetened berries, hot chocolate, pie, Jell-O® or other desserts.

ICE CREAM TREATS

CHOCOLATE CHIP ICE CREAM SANDWICH

Ingredients:
8	large	Deli-style large chocolate chip cookies
1	pint	Vanilla ice cream, softened but firm
1	cup	Miniature chocolate chips

Spread 1/2 cup ice cream on each of 4 cookies; top with remaining cookies. Roll or lightly press ice cream edges into miniature chocolate chips. Freeze until firm, about 4 hours. Wrap in plastic wrap and store in freezer for up to 1 month.

PEANUT BUTTER ICE CREAM SANDWICH

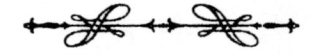

Ingredients:
8	large	Deli-style large peanut butter cookies
1	pint	Chocolate ice cream, softened but firm
1	cup	Peanut butter chips

Spread 1/2 cup ice cream on each of 4 cookies; top with remaining cookies. Roll or lightly press ice cream edges into peanut butter chips. Freeze until firm, about 4 hours. Wrap in plastic wrap and store in freezer for up to 1 month.

COLD DRINKS

LEMONADE

Ingredients:
- 1-1/4 cup   Fresh lemon juice
- 8   cups Water
- 1-1/4 cups Sugar

Combine lemon, water and sugar in a 2-quart pitcher. Stir or shake vigorously until all the sugar is dissolved. Add ice to the top of the pitcher and chill. Serve the lemonade chilled over ice.

STRAWBERRY LEMONADE

Ingredients:
- 2   cups Lemon juice
- 1/2 cup   Strawberry syrup
- 1   cup   Sugar
- 8   cups Water

Mix ingredients together in a pitcher. Serve chilled over ice.

OLD-FASHIONED FLOATS:

ORANGE FLOAT

Ingredients:
1	scoop	Orange sherbet
1	spoon	Orange sherbet
12	oz	Can of orange soda pop, chilled
1	slice	Fresh orange for twist

Place a spoonful of orange sherbet in the bottom of a tall glass, mix with a small amount of orange soda pop. Place a scoop of orange sherbet in the bottom of a tall glass. Fill the glass 3/4 full with orange soda pop, then add a scoop of orange sherbet... sherbet will float. Add an orange slice twist. Serve immediately with a straw.

ROOT BEER FLOAT

Ingredients:
1	scoop	Vanilla ice cream
1	spoon	Vanilla ice cream
12	oz	Can of root beer soda pop, chilled

Place a spoonful of vanilla ice cream in the bottom of a tall glass, mix with a small amount of Root Beer. Fill the glass about 3/4 full root beer, then add a scoop of vanilla ice cream... ice cream will float. Serve immediately with a straw.

BLENDER DRINKS & SHAKES

Shakes:

CHOCOLATE MILKSHAKE

Ingredients:
1	pint	Chocolate ice cream
3/4	cup	Milk
1/2	tsp	Vanilla extract
2	Tbs	Chocolate syrup

Place all ingredients into blender. Blend well until creamy, but still thick. Serves 2

CHOCOLATE COVERED CHERRY MILKSHAKE

Ingredients:
4	Tbs	Chocolate syrup
1	pint	Cherry-Vanilla ice cream
3/4	cup	Milk, chilled
4	each	Chocolate covered cherries

Place all ingredients into blender. Blend well until creamy, but still thick. Serves 2

STRAWBERRY MILK SHAKE

Ingredients:
10	oz	Frozen strawberries in syrup
1	pint	Vanilla ice cream
1-1/2	cups	Milk, chilled

Place all ingredients into blender. Blend well until creamy, but still thick. Serves 3-4

VANILLA MILK SHAKE

Ingredients:
1	pint	Vanilla ice cream
3/4	cup	Milk
1/2	tsp	Vanilla extract

Place all ingredients into blender. Blend well until creamy, but still thick. Serves 2

Slushies:

PEACH SLUSHIE

Ingredients:
- 2 cups Sliced peaches
- 1 Tbs Lemon juice
- 1/2 cup Sugar
- 3-4 cups Cracked ice

Mix peaches, lemon juice and sugar together and place in a blender. Puree until smooth. Gradually add ice until firm. Serve immediately. Makes 4 servings.

LEMON BERRY SLUSHIE

Ingredients:
- 2 cups Strawberries
- 3/4 cup Sugar
- 1/2 cup Lemon juice
- 1 cup Ice water
- 3-4 cups Cracked ice

Mix strawberries, lemon juice, water and sugar together and place in a blender. Puree until smooth. Gradually add ice, pureeing ice and fruit until firm. Serve immediately. Makes 3-4 servings.

PINEAPPLE SLUSHIE

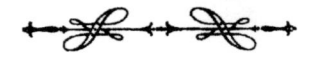

Ingredients:
1	20 oz	Can of pineapple chunks in its own juice
1/4	cup	Sugar
3-4	cups	Cracked ice

Mix pineapple, pineapple chunks with juice and sugar together and place in a blender. Puree until smooth. Gradually add ice until firm. Serve immediately. Makes 3-4 servings.

STRAWBERRY SLUSHIE

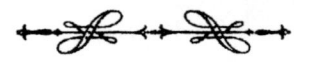

Ingredients:
3	cups	Strawberries
3/4	cup	Sugar
1	cup	Ice water
3-4	cups	Cracked ice

Mix strawberries, water and sugar together and place in a blender. Puree until smooth. Gradually add ice, pureeing ice and fruit until firm. Serve immediately. Makes 3-4 servings.

Smoothies:

BANANA SMOOTHIE

Ingredients:
1	large	Ripe banana
1	scoop	Vanilla ice cream
1	Tbs	Sugar
1	cup	Crushed ice
1	tsp	Fresh lime or lemon juice

Combine the first 5 ingredients in a blender and blend until smooth. Pour the smoothie into a large glass. Serves 1.

PIÑA COLADA SMOOTHIE

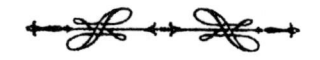

Ingredients:
2	6 oz	Containers of coconut yogurt, frozen
1	large	Banana, frozen
1	20 oz	Can of crushed pineapple, chilled
2	cups	Milk, chilled

Place all ingredients into blender. Blend well until creamy consistency is achieved and no lumps remain. Serves 3-4.

KATE & TYLER METZ with HILDA COOPER

Cutting Up In the Kitchen

What You'll Learn:
- ➤ How to cut, peel, chop and dice foods

What You'll Learn To Use:
- ➤ Sharp knives, vegetable peelers
- ➤ Food processors

Some Safety Issues To Consider:
- ➤ Keep fingers outside of food processors and away form blades; be careful of knives, peelers and other blades
- ➤ Parents or other responsible adults should supervise closely until skills are fully mastered

AMBROSIA

Ingredients:
1	3 oz	Can of sweetened flaked coconut
1	20 oz	Can of crushed pineapple, with juice
1	15 oz	Can of mandarin oranges
15	oz	Can of fruit cocktail
15	oz	Pink grapefruit sections
3	large	Red delicious apples, diced
2	large	Bananas, sliced
1	Tbs	Lemon juice
24	whole	Maraschino cherries

Sprinkle sweetened coconut in bowl. Add pineapple, mandarin oranges, fruit cocktail, pink grapefruit sections, diced apples, sliced bananas, and lemon juice. Sweeten with sugar, if desired; the syrup from the canned fruit is usually sufficient. Chill before serving. Garnish with cherries and serve in a cut crystal or clear glass bowl.

BANANA "POPCORN"

Ingredients:
3-4   large   Bananas

Peel bananas and slice 1/4 to 1/2 inch round slices. Place slices on a foil or wax paper lined tray, cover with plastic wrap and place in freezer for 1-2 hours. When frozen solid, transfer to plastic zip lock bag. Place a few pieces in a bowl and eat like popcorn, frozen. Yummy.

BLT SALAD

Ingredients:

1/2	head	Iceberg lettuce
1	cup	Cherry tomatoes
1/2	cup	Real bacon bits
1/2	tsp	Salt
1/4	tsp	Pepper
1/2	cup	Mayonnaise
1/2	cup	Seasoned croutons

Cut or tear lettuce into small pieces. Cut cherry tomatoes in half. Combine all ingredients except croutons. Toss to mix. Sprinkle with croutons and serve chilled. Yield: 4 servings

CHEF'S SALAD

Ingredients:

1/2	head	Iceberg lettuce
1	cup	Cherry tomatoes
2	Tbs	Real bacon bits
1/2	cup	Ham strips
1/2	cup	Turkey strips
1/2	cup	Shredded cheddar cheese
1/2	cup	Seasoned croutons
1/2	cup	Favorite salad dressing

Cut or tear lettuce into small pieces. Cut cherry tomatoes in half. Combine all ingredients except croutons. Toss to mix. Serve chilled with favorite salad dressing. Yield: 4 servings

CREAM CHEESE & BLACK OLIVE STUFFED CELERY

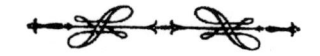

Ingredients:
8	oz	Cream cheese
1	bunch	Celery
1/4	cup	Chopped black olives

Cut celery into 4-inch pieces. Mix softened cream cheese and chopped black olives. Spread on celery. Chill before serving.

CREAMY EGG SALAD

Ingredients:
6	large	Hard-boiled eggs, chopped
1/2	cup	Mayonnaise
1	tsp	Minced onion
1/2	tsp	Salt
1/4	tsp	Pepper
1/2	cup	Chopped celery
2	Tbs	Pickle relish

Combine all ingredients; stir to mix. Cover and refrigerate to blend flavors. Serve on sandwich bread or lettuce leaves. Yield: 4 servings

DEVILED EGGS

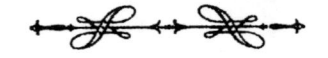

Ingredients:
12	jumbo	Hard-boiled eggs
1/2	tsp	Prepared mustard
1/4	tsp	Seasoned salt
1	Tbs	Pickle relish
4	Tbs	Mayonnaise

Paprika for Garnish

Cut boiled eggs in half-length wise. Carefully remove egg yolks and place in mixing bowl. Set aside. Arrange egg whites on a plate or serving platter and set aside. Add mayonnaise, salt, mustard, (and, if desired, one or more of the optional ingredients according to taste and preference) to egg yolks in mixing bowl, blend until smooth. Spoon or pipe mixture into white halves. Sprinkle with paprika or seasoned salt. Refrigerate until ready to serve.

DEVILED EGGS & HAM

Ingredients:
1	can	Deviled ham sandwich spread
12	jumbo	Hard-boiled eggs
1/4	tsp	Seasoned salt
4	Tbs	Mayonnaise
1	Tbs	Mustard

Paprika for Garnish

Cut boiled eggs in half-length wise. Carefully remove egg yolks and place in mixing bowl. Set aside. Arrange egg whites on a plate or serving platter and set aside. Add mayonnaise, deviled ham, mustard and salt to egg yolks in mixing bowl, blend until smooth. Spoon or pipe mixture into white halves. Sprinkle with paprika or seasoned salt. Refrigerate until ready to serve. Makes 24.

DUCHESS FRUIT SALAD

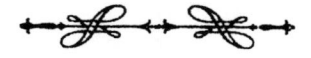

Ingredients
1	cup	Miniature marshmallows
1	cup	Sliced bananas
1	cup	Sliced peaches
1	cup	Sliced strawberries
1	cup	Sour cream

Mix marshmallows, fruit and sour cream in large bowl. Cover and chill until ready to serve.

GUACAMOLE DIP

Ingredients:
2	large	Ripe avocados
1/2	large	Lemon, juiced
2	Tbs	Minced onion
1/2	tsp	Salt
2	Tbs	Olive oil

Cut avocados into halves. Remove the pit, and scoop out the pulp into a small bowl. Use a fork to mash the avocado. Stir in lemon juice, onion, salt, and olive oil. Cover bowl and refrigerate for at least one hour before serving. Serve with corn chips or a variety of raw vegetables. Yield 2 cups

HAM ROLL-UPS

Ingredients:
1	8 oz	Package of sliced sandwich ham
8	stalks	Green onions
1	8 oz	Package of cream cheese

Spread sliced ham with cream cheese. Lay 1 onion along each slice edge and roll up. Chill until cheese is firm. Slice into 3/4-inch pieces and arrange upright on plate. Recipe can be doubled or tripled. Makes 24 appetizer servings.

HAM & CHEESE SALAD

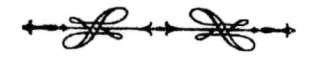

Ingredients:
- 2 cups Chopped ham
- 1 cup Shredded cheddar cheese
- 2 stalks Celery, chopped
- 1/3 cup Mayonnaise
- 1-1/2 Tbs Prepared mustard

In a food processor, combine the ham and celery; pulse until finely chopped. Add cheese and pulse until mixed. Place mixture in a bowl and add the mayonnaise and mustard. Mix well; serve on toast, sandwich or pita bread.

HAPPY PEAR SALAD

Ingredients
- 4 halves Canned pears
- 1/2 cup Shredded cheddar cheese
- 4 Tbs Mayonnaise
- 4 cup Maraschino cherries
- Lettuce leaves

Cover four salad plates with crisp green lettuce leaves. Top each with a pear half. Place a tablespoon of mayonnaise in the concave of the pear half, sprinkle the top with shredded cheddar cheese, and top with a maraschino cherry.

KATE & TYLER METZ with HILDA COOPER

HOLLYWOOD SALAD

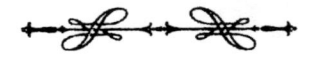

Ingredients:

1/2	head	Iceberg lettuce
1/2	bunch	Watercress
1/2	head	Romaine
2	med	Tomatoes, diced
2	cups	Cooked chicken breasts, diced
1/4	cup	Real bacon bits
1	med	Ripe avocado
3	large	Hard-boiled eggs,
2	Tbs	Chopped spring onions
1/2	cup	Roquefort cheese
1	cup	French dressing

Shred lettuce, watercress, chicory and romaine and arrange in salad bowl. Dice tomatoes and arrange over top of chopped greens. Dice breasts of chicken and arrange over top of chopped greens. Sprinkle bacon bits over the salad. Peel avocado and cut in small pieces and arrange around the edge of the salad. Decorate the salad by sprinkling chopped eggs, chopped spring onions and crumbled cheese over the top. Just before serving mix the salad thoroughly with French dressing.

FRUIT SALAD

Ingredients:
5	med	Granny Smith apples
5	med	Red Delicious apples
1	cup	Pineapple chunks, drained
2	large	Diced bananas
1	cup	Green grapes
1	cup	Chopped pecans
16	oz	Frozen whipped topping, thawed

Core (peel, if desired) and dice the apples. Drain the pineapple and add to diced apples. Add grapes, pecans and whipped topping. Stir until salad is mixed, then chill. Serve chilled.

MONTE CARLO SALAD

Ingredients:

1	bunch	Romaine lettuce
1/2	cup	Black olives
1/2	med	Red onion sliced
2/3	cup	Crumbled feta cheese
2	large	Ripe tomatoes
1/3	cup	Caesar dressing
1/2	tsp	Salt
1/2	tsp	Pepper

Rinse and dry Romaine lettuce. Slice onions and separate into rings. Cut tomatoes into wedges, six per tomato. Tear bite size pieces of clean dry Romaine leaves into salad bowl. Spread black olives evenly across salad, and then arrange red onion rings on top of olives and romaine lettuce. Arrange tomato wedges around edge of bowl and sprinkle fresh crumbled feta cheese across top of everything. Dash with salt and pepper, and serve with Caesar dressing or other favorite salad dressing.

PEANUT MARSHMALLOW APPLE SALAD

Ingredients

1/2	cup	Miniature marshmallows
1	cup	Diced red apple
1	cup	Diced yellow apple
1	cup	Halved red grapes
1	cup	Mayonnaise
1	cup	Peanut butter
1/2	cup	White sugar
1/2	cup	Peanuts
1/2	cup	Raisins
1/2	cup	Diced celery

In a large bowl, whisk together the mayonnaise, peanut butter and sugar until smooth. Add the vinegar, whisking until dressing is creamy. Add additional vinegar to get creamy consistency, if necessary. Add the apples, grapes, peanuts, marshmallows, raisins and celery to the dressing mixture and toss until evenly coated. Serve immediately or chill until ready to serve.

SHRIMP SALAD

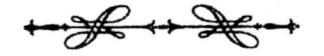

Ingredients:
1/2	head	Lettuce
1	lb	Cooked shrimp
3	large	Hard boiled eggs, diced
1/2	med	Red onion, diced
2	large	Ripe tomatoes, diced
1/2	medium	Green bell pepper, diced
1/3	cup	Honey mustard or French dressing
1/2	tsp	Salt
1/2	tsp	Pepper

Tear lettuce in bite sized pieces. Rinse and dry on paper towels. Combine remaining ingredients, toss with lettuce. Dash with salt and pepper, and serve with honey mustard or French dressing or other favorite salad dressing.

TOMATO SANDWICH

Ingredients:
4	slices	Sandwich bread
1	large	Vine ripe tomato
1-2	Tbs	Mayonnaise

Salt & pepper to taste

Wash tomato, and slice about 1/4 inch thick. Place tomato slices on paper towels. Spread mayonnaise on one side of each piece of bread. Arrange tomato slices on 2 bread slices, top with remaining pieces. Salt and pepper to taste.

TUNA SALAD

Ingredients
- 1   6 oz   Can of tuna, drained
- 1   stalk   Celery, chopped
- 2   Tbs   Sweet pickle relish
- 1   large   Hard boiled egg, diced
- 1/4   cup   Mayonnaise

Salt and pepper to taste

Combine all ingredients in medium sized bowl. Mix thoroughly. Serve immediately on a bed of lettuce, or chill until ready to serve. Makes an excellent sandwich spread, too.

WALDORF SALAD

Ingredients:
- 4   large   Red Delicious apples, diced, peel left on
- 2   tsp   Lemon juice
- 2   ribs   Celery, diced
- 1/2   cup   Mayonnaise
- 1/4   cup   Honey
- 1/2   cup   Seedless raisins
- 1/2   cup   Walnuts or pecans, chopped
- 1/2   cup   Maraschino cherry halves

Toss diced apples with lemon juice. Mix apples with other ingredients. Chill thoroughly. Serve on bed of Bibb lettuce.

DESSERTS:

BANANA SPLIT

Ingredients:
1	large	Banana
1	scoop	Vanilla ice cream
1	scoop	Chocolate ice cream
1	scoop	Strawberry ice cream
1/4	cup	Chopped nuts
1/4	cup	Chocolate or fudge sauce

Whipped cream and maraschino cherries for garnish

Split banana lengthwise; remove the peel. Place in banana split dish or bowl, side by side, cut side up, to form a valley. Fill valley with three scoops of ice cream. Top with fudge sauce (and/or any other ice cream topping you like). Top with aerosol whipped cream, sprinkle with nuts and top it all off with a maraschino cherry. A classic.

BANANA SPLIT CAKE

Ingredients:

2	cups	Graham cracker crumbs
1	15 oz	Can of crushed pineapple
1	15 oz	Container of whipped topping, thawed
1	15 oz	Jar of Maraschino cherries
1-1/2	cups	Confectioners' sugar
3/4	cup	Sugar
1/2	cup	Butter, melted
1	8 oz	Package of cream cheese
4	large	Bananas, sliced
12	oz	Crushed nuts

Combine the graham cracker crumbs, white sugar and melted butter. Mix together and press into a 9x13 inch cake pan; chill for 1 hour. Meanwhile, drain pineapple and cherries; thaw frozen whipped topping. Beat together the cream cheese and confectioners sugar; spread over graham cracker crust. Layer bananas and pineapple over cream cheese mixture; cover fruit with whipped topping. Top with cherries and chopped nuts; refrigerate and serve chilled.

KATE & TYLER METZ with HILDA COOPER

BLUEBERRY OR CHERRY NO BAKE CHEESECAKE

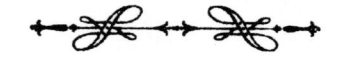

Ingredients:
- 1   9-inch   Graham cracker crust
- 1   8 oz   Package of cream cheese, softened
- 1   14 oz   Can of sweetened condensed milk
- 1/3 cup   Lemon juice
- 1   tsp   Vanilla extract
- 1   21 oz   Can of blueberry or cherry pie filling

Place softened cream cheese in a mixing bowl; add condensed milk, lemon juice, and vanilla. Beat until well blended. Pour mixture into the pie crust. Chill for 5 hours in the refrigerator. DO NOT FREEZE! Pour pie filling on top of pie. Serve chilled.

SUGAR PLUMS

Ingredients:
- 3 Tbs   Orange extract
- 1/3 cup   Confectioners' sugar
- 1/2 cup   Chopped pecans
- 1/2 cup   Prunes
- 1/2 cup   Dried apricots
- 1/2 cup   Golden raisins
- 1/4 cup   Flaked coconut

Finely chop the fruits and nuts (food processor works best). Add orange extract or liqueur; blend well. Shape mixture into 1-inch balls by rolling between palms of hands. Roll each ball in confectioners' sugar. Store in airtight container in refrigerator between sheets of wax paper for up to 1 month.

Microwave Magic

What You'll Learn:
- How to melt butter, chocolate, cheese and other foods in the microwave
- How to cook foods in the microwave

What You'll Learn To Use:
- Microwave oven

Some Safety Issues To Consider:
- Foods and dishes can get very hot in a microwave. Ask an adult to help when taking foods out of the microwave oven, or when stirring or mixing foods in the oven. Be careful of burning steam!
- Parents or other responsible adults should supervise closely until skills are fully mastered

BACON

Ingredients:
4   slices   Bacon

Place two microwave safe paper towels on a microwave safe plate. Place the four strips of bacon on the paper towels, so that they do not overlap. Cover the bacon with a paper towel. Microwave on high for 2-1/2 to 4 minutes, until bacon is done. Using a potholder, carefully remove the plate form the microwave and remove the top paper towel. Using a fork, transfer the bacon to a clean, dry paper towel. Bacon is done and ready to eat.

BACON LETTUCE TOMATO SANDWICH

Ingredients:
4   slices   Bacon
4   slices   Sandwich bread
1   large   Vine ripe tomato
1-2 Tbs   Mayonnaise
Salt & pepper to taste

Prepare bacon as detailed above. Wash tomato, and slice about 1/4 inch thick. Place tomato slices on paper towels. Spread mayonnaise on one side of each piece of bread. Arrange tomato slices on 2 bread slices, top with bacon, and then remaining bread. Salt and pepper to taste.

BAKED POTATO

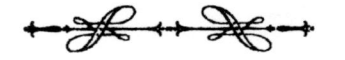

Ingredients:
1   large   Russet or Idaho potato

Butter, sour cream, chives as desired for topping.

Wash the potato, using a vegetable brush to remove all dirt. Place the potato on a microwave safe paper towel, on a microwave safe plate. Microwave on high for 2 minutes, then, using tongs, flip potato over. Microwave another 2 –3 minutes, until a knife is easily inserted in the potato. Allow the potato to cool for 3 minutes. Then split down the center and add butter, sour cream and whatever other toppings you desire.

BARBEQUE BAKED BEANS

Ingredients:
2	15 oz	Cans of pork and beans
1/3	cup	Brown sugar, packed
1/3	cup	Ketchup
1	Tbs	Yellow prepared mustard
1	Tbs	Minced onion, optional
1	tsp	Worcestershire sauce
1/3	cup	Real bacon bits

Combine all ingredients except bacon bits in a 1-1/2 quart casserole dish. Stir to completely mix. Microwave on high for 4-5 minutes. Stir, top with bacon bits, then microwave for another 4-5 minutes. Serve warm.

BROCCOLI TREES & CHEESE WHIZARDS

Ingredients:
1	10 oz	Package frozen broccoli florets
1	8 oz	Jar Cheese Whiz®

Place frozen broccoli in a covered 1-quart casserole dish. Microwave on high for 4-5 minutes. Using a potholder, rotate a half turn and microwave another 2 minutes. Remove covered casserole from microwave and set aside. Remove jar top from Cheese Whiz® and microwave, in jar, on high for one minute. Pour Cheese Whiz® over broccoli and serve.

CHICKEN BAKE

Ingredients:
4	large	Chicken breasts with skin
2/3	cup	All-purpose baking mix
2	tsp	Paprika
1/2	tsp	Salt
1/4	tsp	Pepper

Combine all ingredients except chicken breasts in a plastic storage bag. Seal and shake to mix. Place one piece of chicken at a time in the bag, shake to coat. Arrange chicken skin side up, in an 11 x 7 baking dish, thickest parts to the outside. Loosely cover with wax paper, curl side down. Microwave for 20-25 minutes, turning once or twice during cooking. Chicken is done if juices run clear when cut with a sharp knife.

CHILI & BEANS

Ingredients:
1	pound	Ground beef
2	Tbs	Chili powder
1	10.75 oz	Can of tomato soup
1/3	cup	Water
1	15 oz	Can chili or kidney beans

Break up ground beef in two-quart microwaveable casserole. Microwave on HIGH for 4 minutes, stir and microwave another 3-4 minutes until no pink remains. With potholders, remove bowl from microwave. Stir in remaining ingredients with a wooden spoon. Cover with a paper towel and microwave on high for 5 minutes. Stir again with a wooden spoon, being careful of the hot bowl, and then microwave on HIGH another 5-6 minutes. Let stand in the microwave, turned off, for another 10 minutes. Then, using potholders, remove and serve.

CORN ON THE COB IN HUSK

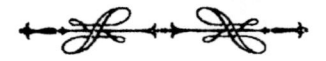

Ingredients:
1	large	Ear of corn in husk

Place ear of corn in husk on a microwave safe plate. Microwave on HIGH for 2-4 minutes. Let stand for 3 minutes. Remove from microwave. Carefully remove husk, watching for escaping steam. Serve immediately with butter, salt and pepper as desired.

CORN ON THE COB, SHUCKED

Ingredients:
1   large Ear of corn, shucked and cleaned

Place corn on a microwave safe plate. Cover corn and plate with plastic wrap. These may take two sheets. Poke several holes in the plastic wrap to allow steam to escape. Microwave on HIGH for 2-4 minutes. Let stand for 2-3 minutes. Remove from microwave. Carefully remove plastic wrap, watching for escaping steam. Serve immediately with butter, salt and pepper as desired.

HOT DOG

Ingredients:
1   whole Hot dog
1   whole Hot dog bun

With a fork, poke a few holes in your hot dog, and then place the hot dog in the bun. Wrap the hot dog and bun loosely in a paper towel or napkin and microwave on High for 25-30 seconds. Let stand for 30 seconds then remove and top with Mustard, ketchup, chopped onion, relish as desired.

LONDON PARTY PIZZAS

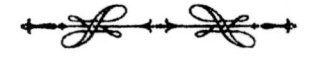

Ingredients:
4	whole	English muffins
6-8	slices	Pepperoni or salami
1	10.5 oz	Jar pizza sauce
1	8 oz	Package shredded mozzarella cheese
2	tsp	Grated Parmesan cheese, optional
1	Tbs	Diced green pepper, optional

Split English muffins and place halves on two microwaveable plates. Top each muffin with 1 to 2 tablespoons of pizza sauce, followed by salami, mozzarella cheese, diced green pepper, if desired, and grated Parmesan cheese. Microwave one plate of mini pizzas at a time on HIGH for 1-1/2 to 2 minutes, until cheese is bubbly. Serve.

NACHO DADDY'S

Ingredients:
16	oz	VELVEETA® Cheese
15	oz	Canned chili (with or without beans)
1	large	Bag tortilla chips

Cut-up Velveeta® into small cubes and combine with chili in 2-quart microwaveable bowl. Place bowl on a large plate and microwave on HIGH 3 minutes and stir to melt and blend. Sprinkle some of the tortilla chips around the bowl. Microwave another 1-2 minutes), stir to blend. Serve hot.

NACHO MAMAS

Ingredients:
- 16 oz VELVEETA® cheese
- 1 cup Salsa
- 1 large Bag tortilla chips

Cut-up Velveeta® into small cubes and combine with salsa in 1-1/2-quart microwaveable bowl. Place bowl on a large plate and microwave on HIGH 3 minutes and stir to melt and blend. Sprinkle some of the tortilla chips around the bowl. Microwave another 1-2 minutes, stir to blend. Serve hot.

SCRAMBLED EGGS

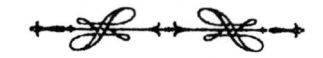

Ingredients:
- 2 large Eggs
- 1 Tbs Milk
- 1 Tbs Butter

Place butter in two-cup microwaveable dish. Microwave on HIGH for 30-40 seconds. Remove; stir to complete melting. Crack eggs in bowl, add milk and whisk until well blended. Microwave on HIGH for 30 seconds, remove, stir with fork and then microwave another 20 seconds. Again remove, stir and microwave on HIGH for 30 additional seconds. Remove from microwave, cover with a paper towel and let stand 2 minutes. Place on plate, and salt to taste. Serve.

KATE & TYLER METZ with HILDA COOPER

SOUTHWEST CHICKEN CASSEROLE

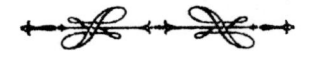

Ingredients:

1	5 oz	Can chicken chunks, drained
1	4 oz	Can diced green chilies
1	10.75 oz	Can cream of mushroom soup
2	cups	Shredded cheddar cheese
2	Tbs	Dried minced onion
1/2	tsp	Salt
1/4	tsp	Pepper
1-1/4	cups	Canned chicken broth
2	cups	Instant rice

Combine the chicken, chilies, soup, cheese, onions, salt, pepper and chicken broth in a large covered casserole dish. Add the rice. Cover the dish with a lid or plastic wrap and microwave for about 15-20 minutes. Allow to cool for five minutes before removing from microwave.

MICROWAVE DESSERTS:

APPLE CRISP

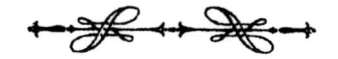

Ingredients
2	large	Tart cooking apples
2	Tbs	Quick-cooking oats
3	Tbs	All-purpose flour
2	Tbs	Packed brown sugar
1	Tbs	White sugar
3	Tbs	Butter, softened
1/2	tsp	Ground cinnamon

Peel and slice 2 medium tart cooking apples; place slices into two microwaveable custard cups or one microwaveable casserole dish. Place on a microwaveable plate for easier handling. Make a topping by mixing the remaining ingredients in a separate bowl small bowl until crumbly. Sprinkle mixture over the apples. Microwave uncovered on high for 5 to 6 minutes, or until the apples are tender when poked with a fork. Using potholders, remove the plate holding the dish or dishes from the microwave oven. Let stand uncovered for 10 minutes to cool. Makes two servings.

CHOCOLATE-PEANUT BUTTER CANDY APPLES

Ingredients:

12	each	Wooden sticks
1	10 oz	Package of peanut butter chips
1	12 oz	Package of semisweet chocolate chips
12	med	Apples
1/2	cup	Solid shortening
1	cup	Chopped peanuts

Wash and dry each apple. Insert a wooden stick into each apple. Line a large pan or tray with waxed paper. In medium microwave-safe bowl, stir together peanut butter chips and shortening. Microwave on high (100%) for 1-1/2 minutes or until chips are softened (chips will not actually melt until they are stirred. They will get soft and shiny). Stir until melted. If necessary after stirring to further melt chips, microwave on high an additional 15 seconds. Stir until thoroughly blended. Dip apples in mixture. While removing the apple from the mixture, twirl to remove excess coating. Set aside on wax paper to harden. In a separate medium microwave-safe bowl, stir together chocolate chips and shortening. Microwave on high (100%) for 1-1/2 minutes or until chips are softened. Stir until melted. If necessary after stirring to further melt chips, microwave on high an additional 15 seconds. Stir until thoroughly blended. Dip peanut butter coated apples in mixture. While removing the apple from the mixture, twirl to remove excess coating. Dip lower half of chocolate coated apple in chopped peanuts if desired. Allow to cool on prepared wax paper lined tray. Refrigerate until eaten.

CHOCOLATE PEANUT BUTTER MARSHMALLOW PUFFS

Ingredients:
2	cups	Semi-sweet chocolate chips
3	Tbs	Shortening
1/2	cup	Peanut butter
1/2	cups	Chopped peanuts
36	large	Marshmallows

Line a 9-inch square pan with buttered foil, allowing foil to extend over the edge of pan. Arrange marshmallows in pan, in six rows each direction. In a microwave-safe bowl, melt chocolate chips, peanut butter and butter on HIGH for 1 to 3 minutes until chips are shiny and beginning to melt. Remove and stir until mixture is thoroughly melted and blended. Quickly pour chocolate over marshmallows; sprinkle with chopped peanuts. Chill completely. Lift foil from pan, cut between marshmallows. Makes 36 candies.

KATE & TYLER METZ with HILDA COOPER

COBBLESTONE SQUARES

Ingredients:
1	12 oz	Package of butterscotch chips
1-1/2	cup	Miniature marshmallows
1	cup	Walnuts, chopped
1	Tbs	Shortening

Grease an 8-inch square pan with wax paper. Combine butterscotch chips and shortening in a large microwaveable bowl and microwave on high for one minute. (chips will not actually melt until they are stirred. They will get soft and shiny) Stir until melted. Microwave on high in additional 15 second intervals if necessary, stirring vigorously after each interval, to complete melting. Do not overcook. Stir in marshmallows and coarsely chopped walnuts. Spread mixture into prepared pan. Refrigerate several hours or until firm. Let stand at room temperature 5-10 minutes before cutting into squares.

FIVE-MINUTE COCOA FUDGE

Ingredients:
1	lb	Confectioners' sugar
6	Tbs	Cocoa
1	12 oz	Semi-sweet chocolate chips
1/4	tsp	Salt
2	tsp	Vanilla extract
1	cup	Butter
1	cups	Chopped pecans or walnuts

Butter and line a 9x13x2-inch pan with wax paper. In a three quart microwaveable bowl, microwave chocolate chips and butter on high for 1-2 minutes, until chips begin to melt (chips will not actually melt until they are stirred. They will get soft and shiny). Stir chips and butter until they are completely melted. Gradually beat in sugar, cocoa, salt and vanilla extract. Microwave mixture on high for an additional 1-2 minutes. Beat vigorously until smooth. Stir in nuts and then pour into pan; refrigerate for one hour, then cut into squares.

KATE & TYLER METZ with HILDA COOPER

HEAVENLY HASH FUDGE

Ingredients:
1	cup	Miniature marshmallows
1	lb	Confectioners' sugar
1/2	cup	Butter
1/4	cup	Milk
3	Tbs	Cocoa
1	tsp	Vanilla
1/2	cup	Chopped nuts

Slice butter and put into a microwaveable bowl with milk and cocoa. Microwave on HIGH for 2 minutes. Stir in sugar. Beat until smooth. Add vanilla and nuts. Microwave on HIGH for 30 seconds. Beat. Add marshmallows and pour into buttered 8-inch square pan. Cool and cut into squares.

MILK CHOCOLATE FUDGE

Ingredients:
- 3 cups Semi-sweet chocolate chips
- 1 14 oz Sweetened condensed milk
- 1 cup Chopped walnuts
- 1/4 cup Butter
- 1-1/2 tsp Vanilla extract

Combine chocolate chips and condensed milk in a microwaveable bowl. Microwave on medium until the chocolate chips are melted, 3 to 5 minutes. Stir twice during cooking to help the melting process. Stir in nuts and vanilla. Pour fudge into greased, 8 X 8 baking pan and chill to set. Cut into one-inch squares.

PEANUT CLUSTERS

Ingredients:
- 1 12 oz Chocolate chips
- 1 12 oz Peanut butter chips
- 1 12 oz Cocktail peanuts

In a large microwave bowl, melt chocolate chips on high for 1-1/2 minutes in a microwave. Pour the peanut butter chips on top of the chocolate and melt for 1-1/2 minutes more. Stir chocolate chips and peanut butter chips together and then stir in peanuts. Drop by heaping spoonfuls onto a buttered non-stick cookie sheet, and let stand at room temp. Makes 40-60 pieces.

PECAN CLUSTERS

Ingredients:
1	cup	Semisweet chocolate chips
2	cups	Miniature marshmallows
2	cups	Pecans

Combine chocolate chips and marshmallows in a large microwaveable bowl. Microwave on HIGH for one minute, stir and microwave on high for another minute stir until the chocolate chips and marshmallows are melted and mixture is smooth. Stir in nuts until well coated; drop by spoonful on waxed paper lined cookie sheet. Chill until firm.

PEANUTTY FUDGE

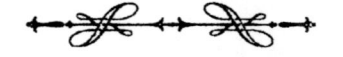

Ingredients:
1	14 oz	Can of sweetened condensed milk
1	cup	White chocolate chips
2	cups	Peanut butter chips
1	tsp	Vanilla extract
1/2	cup	Butter

Combine white chocolate chips, peanut butter chips and condensed milk in a microwaveable bowl. Microwave on medium until the chocolate chips are melted, 3 to 5 minutes. Stir twice during cooking to help the melting process. Stir in peanuts and vanilla. Pour fudge into greased, 8 X 8 baking pan and chill to set. Cut into one-inch squares.

SMORE SQUARES

Ingredients:

3	cups	Semi-sweet chocolate chips
1/3	cup	Light corn syrup
1	Tbs	Butter
1/2	tsp	Vanilla
4	cups	Honey graham cereal
1-1/2	cups	Miniature marshmallows

Combine chocolate chips, corn syrup, butter and vanilla in 3 quart microwaveable covered casserole. Microwave, covered, on high for 3 minutes. Remove from microwave, and being careful of the steam, remove the lid, lifting from the side opposite you. Quickly fold in honey graham cereal, stir until coated and then fold in marshmallows. Transfer to a buttered 9 X 9 baking pan, press down with a large spoon or spatula until the top is fairly even. Chill to set. Cut into 1-1/2 inch squares.

KATE & TYLER METZ with HILDA COOPER

Something From The Oven

What You'll Learn:
- How to bake in a real oven

What You'll Learn To Use:
- Oven

Some Safety Issues To Consider:
- Foods and dishes can get very hot in the oven. Ask an adult to help when taking foods out of the oven, or when stirring or mixing foods in the oven. Always use oven mitts when removing hot pans from the oven. Be careful of steam, and of hot liquids.
- Parents or other responsible adults should supervise Young people closely until skills are fully mastered

BACON & TOMATO CUPS

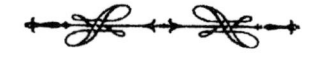

Ingredients:
1/2	cup	Real bacon bits
1	large	Tomato, diced
1/2	large	Onion, diced
1	16 oz	Can of flaky biscuit dough
1	3 oz	Package of shredded Swiss cheese
1/2	cup	Mayonnaise

Preheat oven to 375°F and grease a mini-muffin pan. Crumble crisp bacon into a mixing bowl; mix with tomato, onion, Swiss cheese and mayonnaise. Separate biscuits approximately into halves horizontally. Place each half into cups of the prepared muffin pan. Fill each with tomato-bacon mixture. Bake for 10 minutes or until golden brown.

BAKED BARBEQUE CHICKEN

Ingredients:
6 -8	large	Chicken breasts with skin
1	cup	Barbecue sauce

Wash chicken breasts and place skin side up in shallow baking pan. DO NOT salt or pepper them. Bake in 400°F oven for 25-35 minutes, or until skin is golden brown. Remove from oven. Allow to cool a few minutes and then, using a fork, remove skin and discard. Apply barbecue sauce to skinless chicken and return to oven for 10-15 minutes longer. Do not over cook.

BAKED BEANS

Ingredients:
2	28 oz	Cans of pork and beans
2	small	Onions, minced
1/4	cup	Molasses
1/2	cup	Barbeque sauce
1	Tbs	Liquid smoke

Preheat oven to 325°F. In a 3-quart casserole dish combine beans, onions, molasses, barbecue sauce and liquid smoke flavoring. Bake in preheated oven for 2 to 2-1/2 hours, stirring every 20 minutes

BAKED CHICKEN BREASTS

Ingredients:
4-6   medium   Chicken breasts, with bone and skin

Preheat oven to 450°F. Wash chicken breasts. Place breast side up in roasting pan lined with aluminum foil. Bake at 450°F for 25-35 minutes or until golden brown. If pierced with a sharp knife, juices will run clear. Do not over bake.

BAKED OATMEAL

Ingredients:
3	cups	Rolled oats
1/2	cup	Brown sugar
1/4	cup	White sugar
1/2	cup	Butter
2	large	Eggs
2	cups	Milk
2	tsp	Baking powder
1	tsp	Salt

Mix all ingredients together and pour into 13 x 9 buttered pan. Bake at 375°F for 25 minutes.

BAKED PINEAPPLE

Ingredients:
1	20 oz	Can of pineapple chunks in juice
3	Tbs	Sugar
6	Tbs	Butter, melted
3	Tbs	All-purpose flour
1	5 oz	Package of shredded cheddar cheese
25	each	Buttery round crackers, crumbled

Drain pineapple, reserving 3 tablespoons juice. Combine pineapple, reserved juice, sugar, butter, flour, and cheese. Mix well. Spoon mixture into a buttered 1-1/2 quart baking dish; top with cracker crumbs. Bake at 350°F for 25-30 minutes, or until bubbly.

BAKED POTATOES

Ingredients:
1-4   large   Idaho baking potatoes

Butter, sour cream and chives as desired for garnish

Wash potatoes, scrub with a vegetable brush. Prick skins with fork. Wrap each potato in aluminum foil. Bake at 425°F for one hour. Remove from oven and, with oven mitts or tongs, remove aluminum foil. Slit potatoes halfway through. Fill slit with butter, sour cream and chives as desired.

BARBECUE BABY BACK RIBS

Ingredients:
2   lbs   Pork baby back ribs
2   cups   Barbecue sauce

Tear off 4 pieces of aluminum foil big enough to enclose each portion of ribs. Spray each piece of foil with vegetable cooking spray. Brush the ribs liberally with barbeque sauce and place each portion in its own piece of foil. Wrap tightly and refrigerate for at least 8 hours, or overnight. Preheat oven to 300°F. Bake ribs wrapped tightly in the foil at 300°F for 2-1/2 hours. Remove from foil and add more sauce, if desired.

BARBECUED PORK CHOPS

Ingredients :
6	large	Center-cut pork chops, 1/2 to 3/4" thick
1	tsp	Salt
1/4	tsp	Pepper
3/4	cup	Ketchup or barbecue sauce

Preheat oven to 350°F. Place pork chops in bottom of a 13 x 9-inch baking pan. Bake uncovered for 45 minutes, or until chops are tender. Pour barbecue sauce or ketchup over chops and bake an additional 15 minutes. Serves 6.

BISCUITS

Ingredients:
2	cups	Self-rising flour
1/4	cup	Shortening
3/4	cup	Milk

Heat oven to 450°F. Lightly grease cookie sheet. Place flour in large bowl. With pastry blender or fork, cut in shortening until mixture resembles coarse crumbs. Add milk; stir with fork until soft dough forms and mixture begins to pull away from sides of bowl. On lightly floured surface, knead dough just until smooth. Roll out dough to 1/2-inch thickness. Cut with floured 2-inch round cutter. Place biscuits with sides touching on greased cookie sheet. Bake at 450°F for 10 to 12 minutes or until golden brown. Serve warm.

BROCCOLI-CHEESE CASSEROLE

Ingredients:

2	cups	Instant rice, uncooked
2	cups	Water
4-6	med	Skinless, boneless chicken breast
2	cans	Cream of mushroom soup
2-3	cups	Broccoli florets
3/4	cup	Diced onion
3/4	cup	Diced celery
1	16 oz	Jar of cheese spread
1/2	cup	Melted butter

Thoroughly mix rice, broccoli florets, diced onion, diced celery, processed cheese spread, water and 1-1/2 cans of condensed, undiluted mushroom soup. Place mixture in a buttered covered casserole dish. Place uncooked chicken breasts on top of mixture. Mix remaining soup with melted butter, and brush over chicken breasts. Bake covered at 350°F for 30 minutes. Remove cover and bake an additional 25-30 minutes.

CHEESY RICE CRISPS

Ingredients:
1	lb	Cheddar cheese, shredded & softened
1	cup	Butter, softened
1/2	tsp	Worcestershire sauce
2	cups	All-purpose flour
2	cups	Crispy rice cereal
1/2	tsp	Garlic powder
1	tsp	Salt
1/2	tsp	Cayenne
1/2	tsp	Black pepper

Preheat oven to 350°F. Blend together cheddar cheese, butter, Worcestershire sauce, salt, garlic powder, cayenne pepper, and black pepper in a large bowl. Gradually add in flour and crispy rice cereal. Mix well and form small balls out of the dough. Flatten each ball until the dough is very thin. Arrange the discs on greased cookie sheet. Bake at 350°F for 12 minutes, or until the Cheese Crisps are golden and slightly brown around the edges. Remove from cookie sheet and allow to cool on rack. Store in covered container. Yield 4-5 dozen.

CHILI DOG PIZZA

Ingredients:
2	cups	All-purpose biscuit baking mix
1/2	cup	Cold water
1	7.5 oz	Can of chili
5	whole	Hot dogs sliced thin
1	cup	Cheddar cheese

Preheat oven to 425°F. Mix together biscuit baking mix and water. Stir until a soft ball forms. Roll or pat dough into a 12-inch circle on an ungreased cookie sheet. Pinch the edge of the circle to help form a crust. Spread chili over crust, and then add cheese, and hot dog slices. Bake in the oven for 20 to 25 minutes.

CHICKEN OR TURKEY POT PIE

Ingredients:
1	10.75 oz	Can cream of chicken soup
1	9 oz	Package frozen mixed vegetables
1/2	cup	Milk
1	cup	Cubed cooked turkey or chicken
1	large	Egg
1	cup	All-purpose baking mix

Preheat oven to 400°F. Combine soup, thawed frozen mixed vegetables and cooked chicken or turkey in 9-inch pie plate. Combine milk, egg and baking mix. Pour over mixture. Bake 30 minutes, until golden brown. Serves 4.

CHICKEN & RICE CASSEROLE

Ingredients:

2	cups	Instant minute rice
1	10.75 oz	Can of cream of celery soup
1	10.75 oz	Can of cream of mushroom soup
1/4	cup	Milk
1/2	cup	Water
1	whole	Frying Chicken, cut up
1	pkg	Onion Soup mix

Preheat oven to 325°F. Mix together cream of mushroom soup, celery soup, water, rice and milk. Pour into buttered 8 x 13 inch casserole dish. Arrange chicken on top of rice, skin side up. Sprinkle with onion soup mix. Cover casserole with aluminum foil and baked for 2 hours. Carefully remove aluminum foil, avoiding burning steam, and bake an additional 15 minutes, until golden brown.

CINNAMON TOAST

Ingredients:
6	slices	White bread or raisin bread
1/2	cup	Sugar
2	Tbs	Cinnamon
4	Tbs	Softened butter

Preheat oven to 375°F. place bread on an ungreased cookie sheet. Spread each slice with a thin coat of softened butter. Mix together sugar and cinnamon, and sprinkle about a tablespoon of the mixture on each slice of buttered bread. Place cookie sheet in over for 5-6 minutes or until toast has browned around the edges. Remove from oven and allow to cool for a few minutes before serving.

GREEN BEAN CASSEROLE

Ingredients
1	10.75 oz	Can of condensed cream of mushroom soup
1	can	Crunchy onion rings
2	cans	Green beans, drained
1/2	tsp	Salt
1	dash	Black pepper

Pour condensed, undiluted soup into a quart casserole. Add 1/2 can onion rings, both cans green beans, salt and pepper. Mix well. Bake at 350°F for 20 minutes. Put the other 1/2 can of crunchy onion rings on top of casserole and bake 5 minutes longer.

HAM & CHEESE PINWHEELS

Ingredients:
1/2	cup	Sharp cheddar cheese, shredded
1	8 oz	Can of refrigerated crescent roll dough
1/2	tsp	Prepared mustard
1/2	cup	Ham, chopped
1	large	Egg yolk
1	large	Egg white

Pre-heat oven to 375°F. Combine cheese, egg yolk, mustard and ham in a mixing bowl; stir until well blended. Separate crescent dough into 4 rectangles. Press perforations in dough to seal. Spread about one fourth of the ham and cheese mixture on each rectangle. Start at shortest side and roll up each rectangle. With a sharp knife, cut each roll into 6 slices. Place, cut side down, 1 inch apart on ungreased cookie sheet. Brush with beaten egg white and bake at 375°F until golden brown, about 12-15 minutes. Serve warm.

KATE & TYLER METZ with HILDA COOPER

KID'S BACON & EGG BLENDER KEESH*

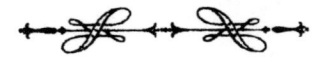

Ingredients:
4	large	Eggs
1	cup	All-purpose biscuit baking mix
2	cups	Milk
1	cup	Shredded cheese
1/3	cup	Real bacon bits

Place eggs, biscuit baking mix and milk in blender and blend for 30 seconds. Grease a 10-inch pie pan or quiche pan and spread cheese over bottom. Pour blended mixture over cheese, sprinkle bacon bits on top and bake at 350 °F for 45 minutes. Filling will puff slightly and be golden brown on top.

Also try these Kid Keesh Variations:

Kid Broccoli Keesh:

Add 1/2 teaspoon Tabasco to ingredients in blender. Layer 1/2 cup cooked broccoli over cheese.

Kid Ham Keesh:

Layer 1/3 cup cubed ham and 1 sliced green onion over cheese.

* Note: Grownups spell Keesh "Quiche"

OVEN FRIED CHICKEN

Ingredients:
6	large	Chicken breasts, skinless
2/3	cup	Bread crumbs
1/3	cup	Parmesan cheese
2	Tbs	Fresh chopped parsley

Italian salad dressing

Mix crumbs, cheese and seasonings in a plastic storage bag. Dip chicken in Italian dressing. Coat with bread crumb mixture. Bake in 350°F oven for 45 minutes.

OVEN FRIED POTATOES

Ingredients:
6	medium	Russet or Idaho potatoes
1	Tbs	Chopped parsley
1	Tbs	Dried basil
1/4	tsp	Garlic powder
1	dash	Pepper
3	Tbs	Olive oil

Spread oil in 13-by-9 inch baking dish. Clean and cut potatoes into wedges or bite sized chunks. Toss potatoes in pan and sprinkle on spices. Put in oven at 375°F for about 60-75 minutes, long enough for the outside to become crunchy and the inside to remain soft. Remove form the oven and serve warm.

PEPPERONI PINWHEELS

Ingredients:
1/2	cup	Shredded mozzarella cheese
1/2	cup	Pepperoni, chopped
1	large	Egg yolk
1	large	Egg white
1	Tbs	Pizza sauce
1	8 oz	Can of refrigerated crescent roll dough

Preheat oven to 375°F. Combine cheese, egg yolk, oregano, pepperoni and pizza sauce in a mixing bowl; stir until well blended. Separate crescent dough into 4 rectangles. Press perforations in dough to seal. Spread about one fourth of the pepperoni mixture-cheese on each rectangle. Start at shortest side and roll up each rectangle. With a sharp knife, cut each roll into 6 slices. Place, cut side down, 1 inch apart on ungreased cookie sheet. Brush with beaten egg white and bake at 375°F until golden brown, about 15 minutes. Serve warm.

PIGS IN A BLANKET

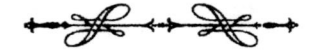

Ingredients:
8	each	Hot dogs
1	8 oz	Can of refrigerated crescent roll dough

Heat oven to 375°F. Separate dough into triangles. Wrap one dough triangle around each hot dog. Place on ungreased cookie sheet, bake at 375°F. for 12 to 15 minutes.

SAUSAGE BALLS

Ingredients:
10	oz	Shredded sharp cheddar cheese
3	cups	Biscuit/baking mix
1	lb	Ground sausage
1/2	tsp	Cayenne

Mix all ingredients together. Form into 1-1/4 inch balls. Bake at 350°F for 20 minutes on an ungreased cookie sheet. Serve warm.

SAUSAGE PINWHEELS

Ingredients:
1	lb	Lean ground sausage
1	8 oz	Can of refrigerated crescent roll dough
1	large	Egg white

Preheat oven to 375°F. Separate crescent dough into 4 rectangles. Press perforations in dough to seal. Spread sausage about $1/8^{th}$ of an inch thick on each rectangle. Start at shortest side and roll up each rectangle. With a sharp knife, cut each roll into 6 slices. Place, cut side down, 1 inch apart on ungreased cookie sheet. Brush with beaten egg white and bake at 375°F until golden brown, about 15-18 minutes. Serve warm.

SOUR CREAM & BUTTER MUFFINS

Ingredients:
2	cups	Self-rising flour
1	8 oz	Container of sour cream
1	cup	Butter, melted

Stir together all ingredients just until blended. Spoon batter into lightly greased miniature muffin pans, filling to the top. Bake at 350°F for 25 minutes or until lightly browned. Yield: 2-1/2 dozen.

TUNA CASSEROLE

Ingredients
2	cans	Water packed tuna, drained
1	can	Condensed cream of celery soup
1	can	Condensed cream of chicken soup
1	cup	Green peas
1/2	large	Onion, chopped
1	cup	Grated Colby cheese
1	cup	Instant rice, uncooked
1/2	cup	Milk
1	tsp	Salt
1/4	tsp	Pepper
1.2	tsp	Garlic powder

Put all ingredients except cheese in buttered casserole dish and mix well. Put cheese on top and cook at 350°F, or about 30 min. or until rice is done.

DESSERTS FROM THE OVEN:

AMAZING PEANUT BUTTER COOKIES

Ingredients:
1	cup	Peanut Butter
1	cup	Sugar
1	large	Egg

Preheat oven to 325°F. Blend all ingredients together. Roll cookies into one-inch balls; flatten with tines of a fork, making a crosshatch pattern. Bake in oven at 325°F for 8 to 10 minutes. Cool before removing from cookie sheet. Cookies will remain soft.

… KATE & TYLER METZ with HILDA COOPER

BANANA NUT BREAD

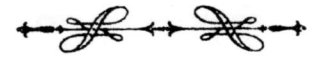

Ingredients:
2-1/2	cups	Sugar
1	cup	Shortening
3	large	Eggs
1-1/2	cups	Mashed bananas
3	cups	All-purpose flour
1-1/4	cups	Buttermilk
1-1/2	tsp	Baking soda
1-1/2	tsp	Baking powder
1	tsp	Vanilla extract
1	cup	Chopped pecans

Preheat oven to 350°F. Cream together shortening and sugar. Add eggs one at a time, beating well after each addition. Mix in bananas, buttermilk, and vanilla. Mix in flour, baking powder, and soda. Stir in nuts if desired. Pour batter into two greased 9x5 inch pans. Bake for 50 to 60 minutes in the preheated oven, or until a toothpick inserted into the center of the loaf comes out clean.

BLUEBERRY MUFFINS

Ingredients:
1-1/2	cups	All-purpose flour
1	cup	Fresh blueberries
3/4	cup	Sugar
1/2	tsp	Salt
2	tsp	Baking powder
1/3	cup	Vegetable oil
1	large	Egg
1/3 +	cup	Milk

Topping:
1/2	cup	Sugar
1/3	cup	All-purpose flour
1/4	cup	Butter, cubed
1-1/2	tsp	Cinnamon

Preheat oven to 400°F. Combine 1 1/2 cups flour, 3/4 cup sugar, salt and baking powder. Pour vegetable oil into a 1-cup measuring cup; add egg and top off with enough milk to fill the cup. Mix this with flour mixture. Fold in blueberries. Fill greased muffin cups right to the top.

Crumb Topping: Mix together sugar, flour, butter, and cinnamon with fork until crumbly; sprinkle over muffin batter before baking.

Bake muffins for 20 to 25 minutes in the preheated oven until done.

KATE & TYLER METZ with HILDA COOPER

BUTTER PECAN BALLS

Ingredients:
- 2 cups Pecans, chopped
- 2 cups All-purpose flour
- 1 cup Butter
- 1/2 cup Sugar
- 2 tsp Vanilla
- 1/2 tsp Salt

Confectioners' sugar for 'dusting' cookies after baking

Cream butter, shortening and sugar until light and fluffy. Gradually beat in flour, alternately adding drops of cold water and vanilla. Finally, mix pecans in with fork. Chill several hours. The colder the dough before shaping and baking the better the final results will be. Preheat oven to 325°F. Shape chilled dough into 1" balls. Place on greased cookie sheet. Bake at 325°F for 15-18 minutes. Let cool for thirty minutes, and then roll in confectioners' sugar. Wait fifteen minutes and roll in Confectioners' sugar again. Allow to dry for a day or two before putting in a container. Makes 6-8 dozen small cookies.

CABANA COOKIES

Ingredients:
- 2 cups Cornstarch
- 1 cup Sugar
- 1 large Egg
- 1/2 tsp Salt
- 3/4 cup Butter
- 1 tsp Almond extract

Preheat oven to 375°F. Cream butter, egg and sugar together. Beat cornstarch, sugar and salt into mixture. Knead well. Chill 10 to 15 minutes. Shape dough into 1-inch balls and place them onto a greased cookie sheet. Press down with fork to make a crisscross pattern. Bake 7-8 minutes at 375°F F until they turn a very light brown. Note: This dough also works well in a cookie press.

CAKE MIX COOKIES

Ingredients:
1	pkg	Any flavor cake mix
2	large	Eggs
1/2	cup	Vegetable oil

Now choose one, two or three of the following:
1	cup	Chocolate chips
1	cup	Peanut butter chips
1	cup	Butterscotch chips
1	cup	M&M's
1	cup	Toffee chips
1	cup	Nuts, chopped
1/2	cup	Coconut
1/2	cup	Raisins

Preheat oven to 350°F. Combine cake mix, vegetable oil and eggs, and mix thoroughly. Stir in one, two or three desired optional ingredients until just mixed. Drop by rounded teaspoons on ungreased cookie sheet and bake at 350°F for 9 - 12 minutes. Makes about 4 dozen cookies

CHOCOLATE CHIP COOKIES

Ingredients:

2	cups	Semi-sweet chocolate chips
1	cup	Chopped walnuts
1	cup	Butter, softened
2-1/4	cups	All-purpose flour
2-1/2	cups	Sugar
2/3	cup	Brown sugar
1	tsp	Baking soda
1	tsp	Vanilla Extract
2	large	Eggs
1	tsp	Salt

Preheat oven to 350°F. In a large bowl, beat together sugar, brown sugar and butter until fluffy. Add eggs and vanilla and beat until thoroughly blended. Combine flour, salt and baking soda. Gradually add flour mixture to butter mixture. Stir in walnuts and chocolate chips. Drop by tablespoonfuls, about 3 inches apart, on a greased baking sheet. Bake at 350°F until the centers are still slightly soft to the touch, 11 to 14 minutes. Makes 2-3 dozen.

KATE & TYLER METZ with HILDA COOPER

CHOCOLATE KISS PEANUT BUTTER COOKIES

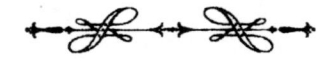

Ingredients:
1	14 oz	Can of sweetened condensed milk
3/4	cup	Peanut butter
2	cups	Biscuit baking mix
1	tsp	Vanilla
1/2	cup	Sugar
36	each	Milk chocolate kisses, unwrapped

Preheat oven to 375°F. Mix milk and peanut butter in large bowl until smooth. Stir in baking mix and vanilla. Shape dough into walnut sized balls and then roll in sugar. Place 2 inches apart on ungreased cookie sheet and bake for 8 to 10 minutes or until bottoms of cookies just begin to brown. Remove from oven and immediately press a chocolate kiss into center of each cookie while cookies are still warm and soft. Allow to cool before serving.

CHOCOLATE KRINKLES

Ingredients:

3	oz	Unsweetened chocolate
1	cup	All-purpose flour
2	tsp	Baking powder
2	tsp	Vanilla extract
1/2	cup	Shortening
1-1/2	cup	Sugar
3	large	Eggs
1/4	cup	Milk

Confectioners' sugar for rolling and dusting

Preheat oven to 375°F. Microwave chocolate and butter in large microwaveable bowl at high 2 minutes or until butter is melted. Stir until chocolate is completely melted. Stir sugar and vanilla into melted chocolate until well blended. Let cool. Beat in eggs, one at a time, beating well after each addition. Beat in milk and then flour and baking powder until well blended. Using a tablespoonful of mixture, shape into balls, roll in confectioners' sugar and place on greased cookie sheet. Bake at 375°F for 10-12 minutes. Let cool for 10 minutes and then remove cookies and roll in confectioners' sugar one more time. Makes 4 dozen cookies.

CHOCOLATE SYRUP BROWNIES

Ingredients:

16	oz	Chocolate syrup
1/2	cup	Butter
1-1/2	cup	All-purpose flour
4	large	Eggs
1	cup	Sugar
1	Tbs	Vanilla extract

Preheat oven to 350°F. Grease 9x13 pan. Beat butter and sugar until well blended. Add flour and beat until blended. Then add eggs, vanilla and chocolate syrup. Blend thoroughly. Pour batter into prepared pan. Bake for 30-35 minutes. Remove from oven and place pan on wire rack to cool. Cut into 24-36 brownies.

CINNAMON MONKEY BREAD

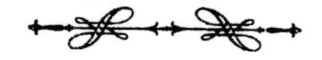

Ingredients:
3	cans	Biscuit dough
2	cups	Sugar
6	Tbs	Cinnamon
1/2	cup	Melted butter
1/2	cup	Chopped pecans

Preheat oven to 375°F. Lightly butter an 8-inch cake pan. Combine sugar and cinnamon in a small bowl, set aside. Cut each biscuit into four pieces; set aside. Dip each biscuit in melted butter, and then roll in cinnamon sugar mixture, and place in pan. Continue the process, placing the biscuit pieces in layers in the pan. Combine the remaining sugar mixture with the remaining butter and pecans. Pour the butter-pecan mixture over the biscuit pieces. Bake in preheated oven for 45 minutes, until top is golden brown.

COCONUT CUSTARD PIE

Ingredients
1/2	cup	All-purpose baking mix
1-1/2	tsp	Almond extract
2	cups	Milk
1	cup	Sugar
4	large	Eggs
1	cup	Coconut
4	Tbs	Butter

Beat eggs. Add milk, sugar, butter, flour and flavorings. Thoroughly mix. Stir in coconut. Pour into greased and floured 10-inch pie pan (no pastry required, pie will make it's own crust). Bake at 350°F for 40-45 minutes or until brown.

COCONUT MACAROONS

Ingredients:
14	oz	Sweetened condensed milk
14	oz	Flaked coconut
1-1/2	tsp	Vanilla extract

Preheat oven to 350°F. In large bowl, beat together coconut, sweetened condensed milk and extracts; mix well. Drop by rounded spoonfuls onto generously greased baking sheets (or pipe from a pastry bag for fancier macaroons). Garnish as desired. Bake 8 minutes or until lightly browned around edges. Cool completely.

FIVE LAYER MAGIC COOKIE BARS

Ingredients:

1/2	cup	Butter
14	oz	Can of sweetened condensed milk
1	cup	Graham cracker crumbs
1-1/2	cups	Semisweet chocolate chips
1-1/2	cups	Butterscotch chips
1-1/2	cups	Sweetened coconut
1	cup	Chopped walnuts

Preheat oven to 350°F. Melt the butter in a 9x13 baking pan. Sprinkle graham cracker crumbs evenly over the butter. Sprinkle on the chocolate chips and butterscotch chips. Cover with flaked sweetened coconut. Sprinkle walnuts on top of the coconut layer. Finally, carefully pour condensed milk over everything as evenly as you can. Bake at 350°F for 30 to 35 minutes. Let cool and cut into 24 squares.

FORGOTTEN KISSES

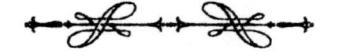

Ingredients:
1/2	cup	Chopped pecans
30	each	Chocolate kisses
1	cup	Sugar
3	large	Egg whites
1	pinch	Salt

Preheat oven to 400°F. Beat the egg whites with the sugar, adding the sugar a little at a time until thoroughly incorporated; add salt and continue to beat until stiff peaks form and hold. Gently fold in nuts. Drop the batter by teaspoonfuls on greased cookie sheet, top with a chocolate kiss and then cover completely with more meringue. Place in pre-heated oven and turn the oven off. Leave in oven at least 6 hours or overnight. Do not open the oven. In the morning, carefully remove puffs from cookie sheet and store in airtight container.

FRENCH APPLE PIE

Ingredients:
3	large	Tart apples, peeled and sliced
1	tsp	Apple pie spice or cinnamon
1/2	cup	All-purpose baking mix
1/2	cup	Sugar
1/2	cup	Milk
1	Tbs	Butter, softened
2	large	Eggs

Streusel
1/2	cup	All-purpose baking mix
1/4	cup	Brown sugar
1/4	cup	Chopped pecans or walnuts
2	Tbs	Butter, chilled

Preheat oven to 325°F. Grease 9-inch pie plate. . Stir together streusel ingredients until crumbly, set aside. Stir together apples, cinnamon and nutmeg; turn into pie plate. Stir remaining ingredients (except streusel) until blended. Pour into pie plate. Sprinkle streusel over top of pie. Bake 40 to 45 minutes or until knife inserted in center comes out clean. Cool 5 minutes. Refrigerate leftovers.

KATE & TYLER METZ with HILDA COOPER

FUDGE BROWNIES

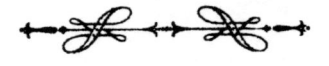

Ingredients:

8	oz	Semi-sweet chocolate chips
1	cups	All-purpose flour
1	cups	Chopped pecans
1	cups	Dark brown sugar
1	cups	Sugar
1	cup	Butter
4	large	Eggs
1/2	tsp	Baking powder
2	tsp	Vanilla extract

Heat oven to 350°F. Completely grease and flour one 9x9x2 inch pans and line with greased parchment. Melt chocolate and butter in a saucepan over low heat. Remove from heat and stir in the sugars and vanilla. Let cool. Add eggs, one at a time, and beat until well blended. Gradually blend in flour and baking powder. Stir in nuts. Pour batter into prepared pan. Bake for 30-40 minutes, until a toothpick inserted in the middle comes out clean or with crumbs. Do not over bake. Remove from oven and place pan on wire rack to cool. When cool, cut into 16 brownies.

MISSISSIPPI MUD PIE

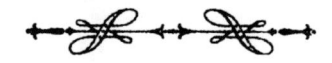

Ingredients:

1	9-inch	Pie shell, unbaked
6	oz	Semi-sweet chocolate chips
1/2	cup	Light corn syrup
1-1/2	cups	Pecans, chopped
1/4	cup	All-purpose flour
1/2	cup	Pecan halves
1	tsp	Vanilla extract
4	large	Eggs, beaten
1/8	tsp	Salt
1/2	cup	White sugar
1/4	cup	Brown sugar
1/2	cup	Butter

Combine eggs, corn syrup, sugars, butter, flour, vanilla and salt in a large mixing bowl; mix well. Stir in chopped pecans and chocolate chips. Pour into pie shell; arrange pecan halves on top. Bake in a 350°F oven 1 hour or until done. Cover edges of pie loosely with foil the last 30 minutes to prevent over-browning.

KATE & TYLER METZ with HILDA COOPER

OATMEAL RAISIN COOKIES

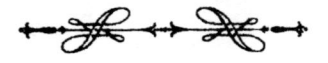

Ingredients:

3/4	tsp	Soda, dissolved in 1 Tbs. cold water
1	cup	Pecans, chopped
2	cups	All-purpose flour
1	cup	Raisins, chopped
1	cup	Sugar
2	large	Eggs
1	tsp	Cinnamon
3/4	cup	Butter
1	cup	Rolled oats

Beat butter, sugar and eggs together until light and fluffy. Gradually stir in remaining ingredients. Drop big spoonfuls of batter for each cookie onto greased cookie sheets. Bake at 350°F for 10-15 minutes.

PEACH COBBLER

Ingredients

2	29 oz	Cans sliced peaches with juice
3/4	cup	Butter
1-1/4	cups	Sugar
1-1/2	cups	All-purpose flour
2	tsp	Baking powder
1/4	tsp	Cinnamon
1	pinch	Salt
1	cup	Milk

Preheat oven to 350°F. Melt butter in 3-quart casserole dish or 9x13 cake pan. Mix all remaining ingredients except peaches thoroughly in a bowl. Pour batter over melted butter; do not stir. Pour peaches and juice over batter mixture. Do not stir. Bake at 350°F for until golden brown and bubbly, about 1 hour. This recipe makes its own crust.

KATE & TYLER METZ with HILDA COOPER

PECAN PRALINE COOKIES

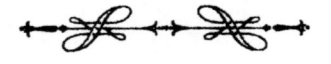

Ingredients:
1-1/2	cups	All-purpose flour
1-1/2	cup	Chopped pecans
1/2	cup	Brown sugar
1/2	cup	Sugar
1-1/2	tsp	Vanilla extract
1	large	Egg, beaten
1/2	cup	Butter

Preheat oven to 350°F. Beat butter, egg, vanilla and sugars together until creamy. Then thoroughly beat in flour. Drop a spoonful of dough for each cookie on ungreased cookie sheet. Bake at 350°F about 10-12 minutes, or until golden brown. Makes 3 dozen cookies.

PUMPKIN PIE

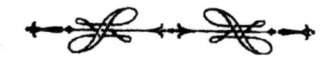

Ingredient:

1	9-inch	Pie shell, unbaked
2	large	Eggs, slightly beaten
1	15 oz	Can of solid packed pumpkin
3	tsp	Pumpkin pie spice
1-1/2	cup	Evaporated milk
3/4	cup	Sugar
1/4	tsp	Salt

Combine filling ingredients in order given and pour into pie shell. Bake in preheated oven at 425°F for 15 minutes. Reduce heat to 350°F. Bake an additional 40-50 minutes or until knife inserted near center comes out clean. Serve with sweetened whipped cream, if desired.

KATE & TYLER METZ with HILDA COOPER

Now You're Cooking

What You'll Learn:
- ➤ How to sauté, simmer, boil & pan fry on top of the stove.

What You'll Learn To Use:
- ➤ Stove top burners

Some Safety Issues To Consider:
- ➤ A kitchen stove is not only versatile, it is dangerous. Be careful of hot burners, hot liquids, and hot pots and pans. Dish cloths and paper towels can catch on fire if they touch hot burners. Never cook on the stove with unless an adult is present. Fire extinguishers are a must. Review kitchen safety procedures with an adult before you begin.
- ➤ Parents or other responsible adults should supervise young people closely until skills are fully mastered

KIDS IN THE KITCHEN

BLUEBERRY PANCAKES

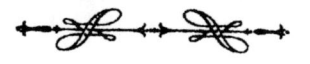

Ingredients:
1	large	Egg
1	cup	Buttermilk
1	Tbs	Oil
1	Tbs	Honey
1	cup	Whole wheat flour
2	tsp	Baking powder
1/2	tsp	Baking soda
1/2	cup	Wild blueberries

Mix together the egg, buttermilk, oil and honey. In a separate bowl combine the dry ingredients with the blueberries. Add together and mix just until it forms a batter. Drop 1/3 cup of batter onto 400-degree griddle. Flip as soon as bubbles form. Cook another 1-2 minutes until golden. Serve immediately with maple or fruit syrup.

CHILI CON CARNE

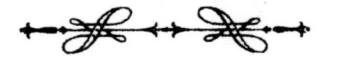

Ingredients:

2-3	lbs	Ground chuck or sirloin
2-3	Tbs	Chili powder
1	diced	Onion
1	tsp	Salt
1	10.75 oz	Can of tomato soup
1	29 oz	Can of diced tomatoes
1	tsp	Prepared mustard
1	29 oz	Can of kidney beans & liquid
1	cup	Water

Brown ground beef in a large saucepan over medium heat. Drain any excess fat. Add onion, salt and chili powder and sauté for about two minutes. Stir in tomato soup and diced tomatoes and simmer for 15 minutes, then add remaining ingredients and simmer for 45-60 minutes, stirring occasionally. Makes 6-8 servings.

CHOCOLATE CHIP PANCAKES

Ingredients:
1/2	cup	Miniature chocolate chips
2	cups	All-purpose biscuit baking mix
1	cup	Milk
2	large	Eggs

Heat griddle or skillet over medium-high heat or electric griddle to 375°F; grease with cooking spray, vegetable oil or shortening. Griddle is ready when a few drops of water sprinkled on it "dance" and then quickly disappear. Stir all ingredients until blended. Pour by 1/4 cupfuls onto hot griddle. Cook until pancakes bubble and edges are dry. Turn; cook until golden, about 1-2 minutes on each side.

FAMILY'S FAVORITE TACOS

Ingredients:
1	pound	Ground beef
2	cups	Shredded lettuce
1	large	Tomato chopped
1	cup	Shredded cheddar cheese
1	cups	Salsa
10	whole	Taco shells

Preheat oven to 350°F. When the oven is hot, place taco shells on a cookie sheet, and warm for 10 minutes or until crisp. Brown ground beef, and drain well. Add salsa to ground beef and heat through. Place in shells with toppings.

KATE & TYLER METZ with HILDA COOPER

GOLDEN CHICKEN & RICE

Ingredients:
1	10.75 oz	Can of cream of chicken soup
2	cups	Cubed baked chicken
1	pkg.	Saffron Spanish or yellow rice (5 oz.)
3/4	cup	White rice, uncooked
2	Tbs	Butter or olive oil
4	cups	Water
1	tsp	Salt

Place cubed chicken along with water, soup, butter and salt in a large heavy saucepan on med-high heat. Bring to a boil, add rices, stir and boil again for 1 minute. Reduce to low heat, cover and, cook for 20 to 25 minutes, being careful to check occasionally to make sure it isn't sticking or the water has not been completely absorbed. After rice is done, you may add a small amount of water, if needed to achieve desired consistency. Serve hot. \

FRENCH TOAST

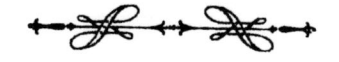

Ingredients:
1	large	Egg
1/3	cup	Milk
4	tsp	Butter
4	slices	Bread

Confectioners' sugar or maple syrup for garnishing

Beat eggs and milk together until well mixed. Melt 1 teaspoon of butter in non-stick skillet over medium heat. Dip bread in egg mixture and brown in skillet about 2-3 minutes each side. Repeat until all four slices are done. Serve with a dusting of powdered sugar and/or maple syrup.

HAMBURGERS

Ingredients:
2	pounds	Ground beef
1/2	cup	Water
1	package	Onion soup mix
8	whole	Hamburger buns
1	Tbs	Olive oil

In large bowl, combine all ingredients; shape into 6 patties. With your finger, make a hole through the center of each burger to speed cooking. Place patties and olive oil in a large skillet, over medium heat. Fry on each side for about 10-15 minutes, or until done. Serve on buns with desired garnishes and condiments.

HARD BOILED EGGS

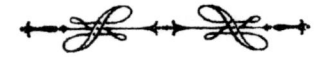

Ingredients:
6   large   Eggs
Water to cover

Put about an inch of cold water in a large saucepan. Carefully place eggs in saucepan and add enough water to cover. Bring water to a boil over medium heat, boil for one minute and then remove form heat. Leave eggs in hot water for 15 minutes. Then pour off water and add fresh cold water. Peel eggs under cold water.

SCRAMBLED EGGS

Ingredients
2   large   Eggs
1   tsp   Milk
1   tsp   Butter

Salt and pepper to taste

Break the eggs into a bowl and whisk or beat with milk until completely blended together. Add salt and pepper. Place a pat of butter in a non-stick pan over medium heat, when butter has melted and begun to lightly brown, pour the eggs into the pan. Let the eggs cook about thirty seconds to one minute, then stir with a wooden or plastic spatula. The eggs are done when they are just dry and there is no moisture left. Serve warm.

PEANUT BUTTER PANCAKES

Ingredients:
1-1/2	cups	Self-rising flour
1/4	cup	Peanut butter
4	Tbs	Sugar
1/2	tsp	Salt
1-1/4	cups	Milk
1/2	Tbs	Vegetable oil
1	tsp	Vanilla extract
2	large	Eggs

Sift together flour, sugar, baking powder and salt in a large bowl. Whisk together milk, vegetable oil, vanilla extract and eggs. Gradually whisk flour mixture into milk and egg mixture, whisking until smooth. Pour a scant 1/4 cup batter onto a hot nonstick griddle or a large nonstick skillet. Turn pancakes when tops are covered with bubbles and edges look cooked. Cook the other side another 1-2 minutes until golden. Serve with a fruity syrup.

TOAD IN THE HOLE

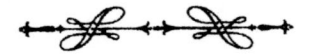

Ingredients
1   slice   Whole wheat bread
1   large   Egg cracked into a small bowl
1   Tbs   Softened butter

Using a 2-inch cookie cutter or a sturdy metal or plastic glass, make a 2-inch hole in the center of the wheat bread. Butter each side. Place a non-stick frying pan over medium-low heat and place the buttered bread in the center of the pan. Wait 30 seconds and pour the egg right into the middle of the hole in the bread. Cook for 2 minutes and then flip over and cook for two minutes more. Flip over again and serve warm.

WAFFLES

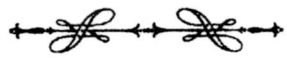

Ingredients:
2   cups   Biscuit mix
1/2   cup   Vegetable oil
2   large   Eggs
1   cup   Club soda

Stir together biscuit mix, vegetable oil and eggs in a large bowl; add club soda, stirring until batter is blended. Cook in a preheated, oiled waffle iron until golden. Makes 8-10 waffles.

STOVE TOP DESSERTS

CRISPY RICE TREATS

Ingredients
1	cup	Mini-chocolate chips
1	10 oz	Package of Miniature marshmallows
1/4	cup	Butter
6	cups	Crispy rice cereal

Melt butter in large heavy saucepan pan over low heat. Add marshmallows and stir until completely melted. Remove from heat   add crisp rice cereal and mini-chocolate chips. Stir until they are well coated. Press mixture into a buttered 13x9x2 inch pan. Allow to cool before cutting into 24 bars.

CHERRY GUMMY GELS

Ingredients
2-1/2	cups	Boiling cherry juice
12	oz	Cherry gelatin

Stir boiling juice into gelatin in large bowl until completely dissolved, about three minutes. Pour into 13x9-inch pan. Chill overnight or until firm. Dip bottom of pan in warm water about 15 seconds. Cut into decorative shapes with cookie cutters all the way through gelatin or cut into 1-inch squares. Lift from pan.

KATE & TYLER METZ with HILDA COOPER

NO-BAKE COCOA OATMEAL COOKIES

Ingredients
2	cups	Sugar
1/2	cup	Milk
1/2	cup	Cocoa
1/4	tsp	Salt
1/2	cup	Peanut butter
1/2	cup	Butter
1	tsp	Vanilla extract
3	cups	Old-fashioned oats

Combine butter, sugar, milk, cocoa, and salt, and bring to a boil, stirring constantly. Boil for 1 minute. Remove from heat and add remaining ingredients. Stir thoroughly and drop by spoonfuls onto waxed paper or foil. Allow to set. Store in covered container. Makes 36-48 cookies.

BLENDER CHOCOLATE MOUSSE

Ingredients:
6	oz	Semi-sweet chocolate chips
2	large	Eggs
1	Tbs	Vanilla extract
3/4	cup	Scalded milk

Set aside 1 tablespoon of the chocolate chips for garnish. Combine the remaining chocolate chips and eggs in the blender. Blend 20 seconds, or just enough to break up the eggs and chips. Heat the milk until very hot but not boiling, then carefully add "scalded" milk to the blender and blend for another 2 minutes. Pour the mixture into 4 small bowls or glasses. Refrigerate until firm (mixture will look thin, but it will firm up). Serve chilled mousse topped with a dollop of sweetened whipped cream and garnish with an extra sprinkling of chocolate chips, if desired.

EASY FAUX FRENCH TRUFFLES

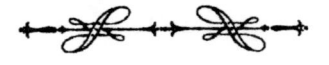

Ingredients:
- 8 oz Unsweetened chocolate
- 4 oz German sweet chocolate
- 1 cup Minced nuts
- 14 oz Sweetened condensed milk

Melt chocolates together in a heavy saucepan over very low heat, stirring constantly until smoothly blended. Add condensed milk and mix until smooth and well blended. Refrigerate for an hour and then shape into one-inch balls. Roll in minced nuts until completely covered. Makes about 4-5 dozen.

FOUR FLAVOR FUDGE

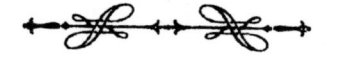

Ingredients:
2	cups	Milk chocolate chips
1	7 oz	Jar of marshmallow crème
1	14 oz	Sweetened condensed milk
2	cups	Semi-sweet chocolate chips
1-1/2	tsp	Vanilla extract
3/4	cup	Butter
1	tsp	Almond extract
2	cups	Peanut butter chips
1	cup	Butterscotch chips
3	Tbs	Milk
1	lb	Walnuts or pecans, coarsely chopped

Melt butter in a heavy stockpot over low heat; stir in sweetened condensed milk and regular milk. Add all chips and stir constantly until all chips have melted and mixture is smooth. Remove from heat; stir in marshmallow cream and flavorings. Stir in walnuts and spread evenly in a buttered 15 x 10-inch jellyroll pan. Chill and cut into squares. Store in the refrigerator. Yields 5 pounds.

KATE & TYLER METZ with HILDA COOPER

PEANUT BUTTER FUDGE

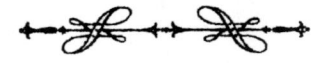

Ingredients:
1	14 oz	Can of sweetened condensed milk
3/4	cup	Peanuts, chopped
3/4	cup	Creamy peanut butter
10	oz	White chocolate chips
1	tsp	Vanilla extract

Line 8-inch square pan with foil, extending foil over edges. Butter foil; set aside. In large saucepan, heat sweetened condensed milk and peanut butter over medium heat until mixture begins to boil, stirring constantly. Remove from heat. Stir in white chocolate until smooth. Immediately stir in peanuts and vanilla. Pour into prepared pan; spread evenly. Cool. Cut into squares and store in a covered container.

KIDS IN THE KITCHEN

WHITE CHRISTMAS FUDGE

Ingredients:
- 3   6 oz   Bags of white chocolate chips
- 1   14 oz   Can of sweetened condensed milk
- 1-1/2   tsp   Vanilla extract
- 1   cup   Pecans, chopped
- 1/8   tsp   Salt
- 1/4   cup   Candied red cherries, halved
- 1/4   cup   Candied green cherries, halved

Over low heat, melt chocolate chips with sweetened condensed milk, vanilla and salt. Stir until thoroughly blended. Remove from heat; stir in cherries and nuts. Spread into foil-lined 9-inch square pan. Chill 2 hours or until firm. Turn fudge onto cutting board; peel off foil and cut into squares. Store covered in refrigerator.

KATE & TYLER METZ with HILDA COOPER

WHITE HOUSE FUDGE

Ingredients:
1-2/3	cups	Evaporated milk
2	cups	Semi-sweet chocolate chips
4	cups	Sugar
2	Tbs	Butter
12	oz	German Chocolate
2	cups	Marshmallow crème
2	cups	Chopped pecans
1	tsp	Vanilla extract

Butter a 9x13-inch pan and the sides of a heavy 2-quart saucepan. Combine milk, butter, sugar and salt. Stirring constantly, cook over moderate heat bring to a vigorous boil, then reduce heat and simmer for 6 minutes. Place remaining ingredients (except nuts) in a mixing bowl. Pour boiling syrup over chocolate marshmallow mixture, beating until melted. Allow to cool slightly, then beat until fudge begins to thicken and lose its gloss. Stir in nuts. Immediately spoon out into buttered pan. Cut into squares when the fudge is absolutely firm.

Master Kid Chef

What You'll Learn:
- How to put all your skills together to make more complicated recipes. You are now on your way!

What You'll Learn To Use:
- Your brain and more complicated recipes!

Some Safety Issues To Consider:
- Just because you know ho to cook now, do not think the kitchen is no longer dangerous. Knives still cut, glass still breaks, foods can boil over, and things can catch on fire in just a few seconds. Until you are a young adult, you still need and adult close by. You need to review safety procedures with an adult frequently and you need to know how to find and use the fire extinguisher. Good luck and happy cooking!

KATE & TYLER METZ with HILDA COOPER

EGGPLANT PARMESAN

Ingredients:

3	med	Eggplant, peeled and thinly sliced
2	large	Eggs, beaten
4	cups	Italian breadcrumbs
6	cups	Spaghetti sauce, divided
1	lb	Package of shredded mozzarella cheese, divided
1/2	cup	Grated Parmesan cheese, divided

Dried basil leaves to taste

Preheat oven to 350°F. Dip eggplant slices in egg, then in bread crumbs. Place in a single layer on a baking sheet. Bake in preheated oven for 5 minutes on each side. In a 9x13 inch baking dish spread spaghetti sauce to cover the bottom. Place a layer of eggplant slices in the sauce. Sprinkle with mozzarella and Parmesan cheeses. Repeat with remaining ingredients, ending with the cheeses. Sprinkle basil on top. Bake in preheated oven for 35 minutes, or until golden brown.

HEARTY BEEF VEGETABLE SOUP

Ingredients:
2	lbs	Stew meat, diced
1	large	Onion, chopped
1	15 oz	Can of diced tomatoes
1	46 oz	Can of spicy-hot V-8® vegetable juice
1	29 oz	Can of home style large cut Veg-all®
2	15 oz	Cans of yellow corn
2	15 oz	Cans of green peas
2	Tbs	Olive oil
1	quart	Water
1	Tbs	Sugar

Salt & pepper to taste

Place olive oil and onions in the bottom of a very large stockpot. Place over medium high heat and sauté until onions begin to brown. Add stew meat and brown. Add, water, diced tomatoes, and V-8 Spicy juice®. Cook 2-3 hours, until stew meat is fork tender. Add remaining ingredients. Cover securely and cook another 20-30 minutes. Serve hot. Makes 10-12 servings. Refrigerate leftovers.

INDIVIDUAL FANCY MEATLOAVES

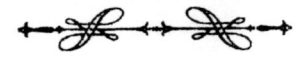

Ingredients:

2	lbs	Ground beef
2	cups	Crushed cornflakes
1-1/2	cups	Ketchup
1	large	Bell pepper, diced
2	large	Onions, diced
1	Tbs	Yellow mustard
1	tsp	Salt
1/4	tsp	Black pepper
6	large	Eggs, beaten
1/2	cups	Ketchup for topping

Mix all ingredients (except ketchup) together gently. Form into eight to twelve individual loaves and place in large baking pan. Bake at 350°F for about 30 minutes. Remove from oven and top each meatloaf with ketchup. Return to oven for an additional 10-15 minutes. Makes 8-12 servings.

LASAGNA

Ingredients:
- 4 cups   Tomato-basil pasta sauce
- 6 noodles   Uncooked lasagna
- 1 10 oz   Package of shredded mozzarella
- 1 lb   Ground beef
- 1 15 oz   Package of Ricotta cheese
- 1/4 cup   Hot water

Sauté beef over medium heat, stirring until it crumbles and is no longer pink. Drain excess fat and then stir in pasta sauce. Spread one-third of meat sauce in a lightly greased 11x7-inch baking dish; layer with 3 noodles and half each of ricotta cheese and mozzarella cheese. Repeat procedure and then cover with remaining meat sauce. Trickle about 1/4 cup hot water around inside edge of dish. Tightly cover baking dish with heavy-duty aluminum foil and bake at 375°F for 45 minutes; then uncover and bake 10 more minutes.

KATE & TYLER METZ with HILDA COOPER

MACARONI & CHEESE

Ingredients:
2	cups	Elbow macaroni
3/4	cup	Shredded cheddar cheese
6	oz	Velveeta cheese
9	cups	Water
3	Tbs	Whole milk
1/2	tsp	Salt

Bring water to a boil in a medium saucepan over high heat. Add elbow macaroni to boiling water and cook it for 10 to 12 minutes or until tender, stirring occasionally. While the macaroni is boiling, prepare the cheese sauce by combining the remaining ingredients in a small saucepan over low heat. Stir often as the cheese melts into a smooth consistency. When the macaroni is done, pour into a colander to drain water and then place it back into the same pan, without the water. . Add the cheese sauce to the pan and stir gently until the macaroni is well coated with the cheese. Serve immediately while hot.

MAPLE GLAZED BABY CARROTS

Ingredients:
1	lb	Baby carrots
1/4	cup	Pure maple syrup
1/4	cup	Brown sugar
1/4	cup	Honey Mustard

Boil or steam baby carrots until tender. While carrots are cooking, in saucepan mix together maple syrup, brown sugar and honey mustard marinade. Cook until mixture is thickened. Pour over cooked carrots and serve.

MAPLE-GLAZED YAMS & CRANBERRIES

Ingredients:
2	tsp	Grated orange peel
5	lbs	Sweet potatoes peeled, cut into 1-inch pieces
1	cup	Maple syrup
6	Tbs	Butter, melted.
6	Tbs	Dried cranberries

Preheat oven to 350°F. Cook yams in large pot of boiling salted water 3 minutes. Drain; transfer to 13x9x2-inch glass baking dish. Blend syrup, butter and orange peel in small bowl. Pour over yams, toss to coat. Cover and bake at 350°F for 40 minutes. Uncover and continue baking for about 15 minutes, or until potatoes are tender and syrup is bubbling hot.

KATE & TYLER METZ with HILDA COOPER

SWEET POTATO SOUFFLÉ

Ingredients:

1	14.5 oz	Can of Sweet potatoes, mashed
1/3	cup	All-purpose flour
3	large	Eggs, lightly beaten
3/4	cup	Sugar
1/2	cup	Brown sugar
1/4	cup	Milk
1	tsp	Orange zest
3	Tbs	Orange juice
1	tsp	Vanilla extract
1/4	cup	Butter, melted

Topping:

1	cup	Chopped pecans
1/3	cup	All-purpose flour
1	cup	Brown sugar
1/4	cup	Butter

Beat together all ingredients for the soufflé until light and fluffy. Pour into a lightly greased 13- x 9-inch baking dish or a 9-inch soufflé dish. . Prepare topping by combining pecans, brown sugar, flour, and butter; sprinkle evenly over potato mixture. Bake at 350°F for 40 minutes or until bubbly. Serve warm.

TUNA NOODLE CASSEROLE

Ingredients

1	12 oz	Package of medium egg noodles
2	7 oz	Cans of tuna
1/2	cup	Minced onion
1-1/2	cups	Diced celery
1	cup	Mayonnaise
1/4	cup	Diced pimiento
3/4	tsp	Salt
1	10.75 oz	Can of cream of shrimp or chicken
1	10.75 oz	Can of cream of celery soup
1	cup	Milk
1-1/2	cups	Shredded cheddar cheese

Combine noodles with tuna, onion, celery, mayonnaise, pimiento, and salt. Mix soup and milk together in a 2-quart saucepan over medium low heat until heated through. Add cheese and stir until smooth and cheese is melted. Pour over noodle mixture and stir to combine. Pour into two 2-quart greased casseroles; bake at 375°F for about 45 minutes. Serves 8 to 10.

TURKEY CHILI

Ingredients:

1	lb	Ground turkey
1	cup	Chopped onion
3	Tbs	Olive oil or butter
1/2	cup	Diced green pepper
2	15 oz	Cans of diced tomatoes
2	7 oz	Cans of tomato sauce
3	Tbs	Chili powder
1	clove	Garlic, minced
1	whole	Jalapeno pepper
1	15 oz	Can of chili beans

Cook olive oil, onion and turkey in a large saucepan until meat is browned. Add chili powder and remaining ingredients except beans, stir well; bring to a boil. Cover; reduce heat, and simmer, stirring occasionally, 1 hour and 30 minutes to 2 hours. Add beans, stirring well, and cook until thoroughly heated. Serves 6.

MASTER KID CHEF DESSERTS

ALL AMERICAN POUND CAKE

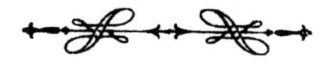

Ingredients:
3-1/2	cups	All-purpose flour
8	large	Eggs
2	cups	Butter
2	cups	Sugar
2	Tbs	Vanilla extract
1	Tbs	Lemon extract

Preheat oven to 325°F. Grease and flour large tube pan, or two loaf pans. Beat butter until soft and creamy. Gradually add sugar, beating until fluffy. Add eggs, one at a time, beating until yellow disappears and mixture is light and fluffy. Add vanilla, and mix well. Gradually add flour to creamed mixture, just until blended after each addition. Pour into prepared pan and bake for 1 hour and 20 minutes or until wooden pick inserted in center comes out clean. Cool in pan on a wire rack for 10 to 15 minutes; remove from pan and let cool completely on wire rack.

APPLESAUCE-SPICE POUND CAKE

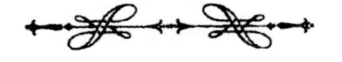

Ingredients:

1	cup	Butter, softened
1-1/2	cups	Brown sugar, packed
1-1/2	cups	Sugar
5	large	Eggs
1-1/2	cups	Applesauce
2	tsp	Baking soda
3	cups	All-purpose flour
2	tsp	Apple pie spice
1	cup	Pecans, chopped
1	cup	Raisins

Preheat oven to 325°F. Grease and flour large tube pan. Beat butter about two minutes, or until soft and creamy. Gradually add sugars, beating until fluffy. Add eggs, one at a time, beating just until yellow disappears. Combine applesauce and baking soda; set aside. Combine 2-3/4 cups flour and spices; add to butter mixture alternately with applesauce mixture, beginning and ending with flour mixture. Mix just until blended after each addition. Combine remaining flour with raisins and pecans; then fold into batter. Pour batter into prepared pan. Bake at 325°F for 1 hour and 15 to 20 minutes or until a wooden pick inserted in center comes out clean. Cool in pan on a wire rack 10 to 15 minutes; remove from pan, and let cool completely on a wire rack.

CARROT CAKE & CREAM CHEESE FROSTING

Ingredients:
Cake:
1-1/2	cups	Shortening
2	cups	All-purpose flour
3	cups	Grated raw carrots
1/2	cup	Walnuts, chopped
4	large	Eggs
2	cups	Sugar
2	tsp	Baking powder
2	tsp	Baking soda
3	tsp	Cinnamon
1	tsp	Salt

Frosting:
1	16 oz	Box of Confectioners' sugar
1/2	cup	Butter, softened
1	8 oz	Package of cream cheese
1	tsp	Vanilla
1/2	cup	Walnuts, chopped

Preheat oven to 350°F. Grease and flour three 9-inch round cake pans. In large bowl, beat eggs and shortening. Combine dry ingredients in separate bowl. Add to egg and shortening mixture. Beat well. Add carrots and walnuts. Blend. Pour into prepared pans. Bake in 350° oven for 25 minutes. Let cake layers cool in pan and remove to platter. To make frosting, combine confectioners' sugar, cream cheese, butter, and walnuts. Spread on cake. Refrigerate until ready to serve.

KATE & TYLER METZ with HILDA COOPER

CHOCOLATE ICED YELLOW LAYER CAKE

Ingredients:

2	cups	All-purpose flour
2	tsp	Baking powder
3/4	tsp	Salt
1-1/2	cups	Sugar
1/3	cup	Shortening
1/3	cup	Butter, softened
3/4	cup	Milk
1	tsp	Vanilla
3	large	Eggs

Frosting:

8	Tbs	Butter, softened
4	cups	Confectioners' sugar
2/3	cup	Cocoa
1/3	cup	Cream
1-1/2	tsp	Vanilla extract

Preheat oven to 350°F. Grease and flour three 9-inch round cake pans. Sift flour, baking powder, and salt together. Add remaining ingredients to flour mixture, beat until thoroughly mixed. Pour batter into prepared pans. Bake at 350°F for 20 to 25 minutes or until cake begins to pull away from sides of pans and toothpick inserted in center comes out clean. To make frosting, beat butter and confectioners' sugar until fluffy. Add cocoa alternately with cream; beating until a good spreading consistency is achieved. (Additional cream may be needed).

DEVIL'S FOOD CAKE

Ingredients
2	cups	All-purpose flour
1	tsp	Baking soda, dissolved in 1 Tbs. warm water
2	cups	Sugar
2/3	cup	Butter
1	tsp	Salt
4	tsp	Vanilla extract
1	cup	Cold coffee
4	large	Eggs, separated
2/3	cup	Cocoa, sifted

Frosting:
4	cups	Confectioners' sugar
1	large	Egg white, beaten
2/3	cup	Sifted cocoa
1	tsp	Vanilla extract
5	tsp	Hot coffee
3/4	cup	Butter
1/8	tsp	Salt

Preheat oven to 325°F. Grease and flour three 9-inch cake pans. Cream sugar, butter and 4 egg yolks. Sift together flour, salt and cocoa. Add coffee, vanilla, and soda. Add flour mixture to sugar mixture. Beat egg whites and add to mixture. Pour into 3 cake pans and bake at 325°F for 25 minutes. Frosting: Sift together confectioners' sugar, cocoa, and salt. Beat egg whites and then add vanilla, hot coffee and butter. Combine sugar mixture and egg mixture. Mix well and spread between layers and on sides and top of cake.

DOUBLE-DIPPED GOURMET APPLES

Ingredients:
2	cups	Semi-sweet chocolate chips
1	Tbs	Solid shortening
1	cup	Chopped pecans
5	med	Apples
5	each	Wooden sticks
48	each	Caramels

Wash and dry each apple. Insert a wooden stick into each apple. Line a large pan or tray with waxed paper. In medium microwave-safe bowl, microwave caramels on HIGH for 1-1/2 minutes or until caramels are softened. Stir until melted. If necessary after stirring to further melt caramels, microwave on high an additional 15 seconds. Stir until thoroughly melted. Do not overcook. Dip apples in caramels and set aside to harden. Next day, in medium microwave-safe bowl microwave chocolate chips and shortening on HIGH for 1 minute or until chips are softened Stir until melted. If necessary after stirring to further melt chips, microwave on high an additional 15 seconds. Dip caramel apples into melted chocolate, leaving some caramel exposed. While removing the apple from the chocolate mixture, twirl to remove excess coating. Dip lower half of coated apple in chopped pecans. Allow to cool on prepared tray.

KEY LIME PIE SQUARES

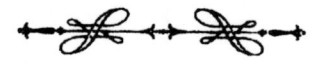

Ingredients:
Crust:
1/2	cup	Confectioners' sugar
2	cup	All purpose flour
1	cup	Butter

Filling:
6	Tbs	Key lime juice
1	tsp	Baking powder
4	large	Eggs; beaten
4	Tbs	Flour
2	cup	Sugar
1	pinch	Salt

Confectioners' sugar for dusting

Preheat oven to 350°F. Mix crust ingredients together and pat into a 13x9x2-inch pan. Bake at 350°F for 15-18 minutes. Meanwhile, prepare the filling. Beat together the eggs, sugar and lime juice. Beat in the flour, salt, and baking powder. Pour on top of the crust. Bake at 350°F for 25 minutes. Cool completely. Sprinkle the top with confectioners' sugar and cut into 24 bars.

LEMON CAKE

Ingredients:

3/4	cup	Butter, softened
1	tsp	Grated lemon rind
1	tsp	Lemon juice
1-1/4	cups	Sugar
8	large	Egg yolks
2-1/2	cups	Cake flour
3	tsp	Baking powder
1/4	tsp	Salt
3/4	cup	Milk
1	tsp	Vanilla extract

Lemon Frosting:

4	cups	Confectioners' sugar
4	Tbs	Lemon juice
1/2	cup	Butter, softened
2	Tbs	Grated lemon rind
4	tsp	Cream

Preheat oven to 350°F. Grease and flour three 9-inch round cake pans. Cream butter and sugar until fluffy. Beat egg yolks until light and lemon-colored; blend into creamed mixture. Sift together flour, baking powder and salt; resift 3 times. Add to creamed mixture in thirds, alternating with milk; beating thoroughly after each addition. Add vanilla extract, lemon rind and lemon juice; beat 2 minutes. Bake in three greased 9-inch round cake pans at 350°F for 25 minutes. Frosting: Combine all ingredients except cream and beat until smooth. Add cream as needed to reach spreading consistency. Spread on cake.

LEMON MERINGUE PIE

Ingredients
2	drops	Yellow food coloring
1	9-inch	Baked pastry shell
1/2	cup	Lemon juice
1	14 oz	Can of sweetened condensed milk
3	large	Eggs yolks

Meringue:
3	large	Egg whites
1/4	tsp	Cream of tartar
1/2	cup	Sugar

Preheat oven to 350°F. In medium bowl, beat together egg yolks, sweetened condensed milk, lemon juice and food coloring. Pour into prepared pastry shell. In a separate bowl, beat egg whites with cream of tartar until soft peaks form; gradually add sugar, beating until stiff and glossy, but not dry. Spread on top of pie, sealing carefully to edge of shell. Bake in 350°F oven for 12 to 15 minutes or until meringue is golden brown. Cool. Chill before serving. Refrigerate leftovers.

KATE & TYLER METZ with HILDA COOPER

LEMON PIE SQUARES

Ingredients:
Crust:
2   cups   All-purpose flour
1/2   cup   Confectioners' Sugar
1   cup   Butter

Filling:
4   Tbs   All-purpose flour
1   tsp   Baking powder
4   large Eggs
2   cups   Sugar
1   pinch Salt
6   Tbs   Lemon juice
1   Tbs   Lemon zest

Confectioners' sugar

Preheat oven to 350°F. To make crust, sift together flour and confectioners' sugar; cut in butter. Press evenly into ungreased glass 8 x 12 casserole. Prick with fork. Bake 15-20 minutes, until just golden. Reduce oven to 325°F. For filling, mix eggs, sugar, flour, baking powder, salt, lemon juice and zest. Pour filling over crust and bake 30 minutes. Dust with confectioners' sugar while still warm. Chill until completely set. Cut in 1-1/2 inch squares.

PEANUT BUTTER BUCKEYES

Ingredients:
1-1/2	cup	Chunky peanut butter
1	lb	Box of confectioners' sugar
1/2	cup	Butter
1	Tbs	Vanilla extract

Chocolate Coating
1	8 oz	Bag of semisweet chocolate chips
1	block	Paraffin
1/4	cup	Shortening

Beat together peanut butter, butter and vanilla. Gradually add confectioners' sugar. Roll into balls. In a microwaveable container, combine chocolate chips, paraffin and shortening. Microwave on high for one and a half minutes. Stir until melted chips and shortening are completely blended. Microwave on high in additional 15 second intervals if necessary to complete melting, stirring well between each interval. Do not overcook. Using toothpicks or cocktail fork, dip balls into chocolate mixture, set on waxed paper to cool.

PUMPKIN ICED BLONDIES

Ingredients:

2-1/4	cups	All-purpose flour
2-1/2	tsp	Baking powder
3/4	cup	Butter, softened
2	tsp	Cinnamon
1	cup	Pumpkin, mashed
1/4	tsp	Salt
1-1/2	cups	Brown sugar
1	tsp	Vanilla extract
2	large	Eggs

Vanilla Icing:

2	cups	Confectioners' sugar
2	Tbs	Butter, softened
1	8 oz	Package of cream cheese
1	tsp	Vanilla extract

Preheat oven to 350°F. Grease 15 x 10-inch jellyroll pan. Combine flour, baking powder, cinnamon and salt in medium bowl. Beat sugar, butter and vanilla extract in a large bowl. Add eggs one at a time, beating well after each addition. Beat in pumpkin. Gradually beat in flour mixture. Spread into prepared pan. Bake at 350°F for 20 to 25 minutes or until wooden pick inserted in center comes out clean. Cool completely in pan; spread with vanilla icing. Cut into bars. Vanilla Icing: Beat cream cheese, butter, vanilla extract and confectioners' sugar in small bowl until smooth

Printed in the United States
4161